BETRAYED IN WONDERLAND

WONDERLAND CHRONICLES
BOOK THREE

FoxTales Press

DANI HOOTS

Betrayed in Wonderland
Wonderland Series, #3
© 2021 FoxTales Press
Content edits by: Nightingale Proofreading
Proofreading by: Victory Editing
Cover Design Copyright © 2020 by Biserka
Designs
All rights reserved.

ISBN for paperback: 978-1-942023-79-1

ISBN for hardcover: 978-1-942023-80-7

"One of the deep secrets of life is that all that is really worth the doing is what we do for others."

— Lewis Carroll

CHAPTER ONE

I glanced down at my notebooks for the term, all of them labeled Junior Year: Fall Term, as I took them out of my backpack. I couldn't believe how fast the spring and summer seasons went. I spent most of my summer in the real world, as traveling to Wonderland felt a bit off with Malcolm and me in a friend zone. Both of us didn't say much to each other, and I tried my best to work around him the few times I had visited. During those times, I didn't really see Malcolm, but instead Chase taught me more about the Dark Forest. I doubted I really needed to worry about the area any longer, but I'd rather be prepared than kick myself later. Again.

So far Malcolm and Bill hadn't found anything on Morpheus or who could have been helping him. Melvin and Davis spent most of the summer in Wonderland as well, and Chase kept me entertained, along with ballet practice. They also still weren't sure how Morpheus was able to travel to this world, so Chase stayed behind in case there was another attack on me. It was nice to not be completely alone, but it was still strange to be without the others. Especially Malcolm.

I did spend a lot of time with Kate this summer, however, and we went through college-application requirements together and even toured a few colleges in Oregon. I wasn't sure where I wanted to go, and the idea of going to college when there was still everything happening in Wonderland was a bit complex. I didn't know what I wanted to do yet, and I couldn't explain it to anyone around me as they would just think I was crazy. So I kept acting like I wanted to go to an art school and started saving up my allowance. So far I had $145.89. That would get me far at a specialized school, right? My parents had a college savings fund for me, but I wasn't sure how my going to an art school was going to play out, so I decided I should start saving up just in case.

Kate took a seat next to me in AP European history class. My parents insisted I take at least two AP classes this year, so I was taking this and AP biology. I figured

AP biology wouldn't be too bad, especially since Chase was taking it with me and we could be lab partners, and for AP European history, we got the option of traveling to Europe this Thanksgiving break. Granted, we had to write a ten-page paper on what we learned, but I figured it was worth it.

It was the first day of school, however, so I would find out how hard these classes truly were as we would be going over the syllabus during class. I had a feeling this evening would include a lot of crying and painting my worries away.

"So," Kate began as she pulled out her color-coordinated notebook and pencil. "I notice you've been wearing those floral dresses more often. They're quite cute on you."

I glanced down at my dress. I was wearing the one the farmer's wife, Penny, had given me. I felt it was good luck since they'd helped me get back to the palace. I definitely needed luck today.

"Yeah, they're pretty comfortable, and the design makes it hard to notice any paint stains."

She pointed at a spot on the sleeve. "You mean like right here? Or right here?"

My face turned red. "Crap, really?"

Kate laughed. "It's not noticeable. I'm just used to being able to point out your stains. Believe me, no one will see it."

I tried to feel reassured, but I still had some doubts. This was not a great feeling to have my first day of school. At least now I didn't have to worry about Lilith making me feel worse after school as she had moved out and was now going to Oregon State University on a scholarship for physics or something like that. I just knew that there was no way I would go to OSU as I didn't want to run into her. That and the thought of being closer to the town of Eddyville gave me the creeps.

The bell rang and Mr. Lewis closed the classroom door as a couple of students hurried through it at the last second. "All right, class. Today we will be mostly going over the syllabus and over any questions you might have for the year and the field trip later this term. I will be sending a note home with all the details of the trip, including fees, so please give it to your parents so that they are made aware."

Mr. Lewis started handing out thick stacks of paper that had been stapled together. "This is your syllabus. Take one and pass it down. It has all the assignments and schedule of quizzes and tests for the year. This next packet is the information on the trip."

I took a syllabus and tried not to start hyperventilating. This was huge. How many trees died to make this? I gulped as I flipped through it. This was going to be a lot of work. I couldn't even grasp how Mr.

Lewis thought we would be able to juggle this, our other classes, and extracurricular activities.

Kate patted my back. "It will be fine. Deep breaths. We will be in this together."

I slowly nodded, but that didn't change the fact that this was going to impede my art time. Maybe I could bring my art supplies to Wonderland and paint there since time slowed down in this world while I was there. It was strange, especially when I was in my world, it matched to the same time. Wibbly-wobbly, timey-wimey stuff, I supposed. It made it very convenient, however. Otherwise, years would have passed in Wonderland and they would have already moved on without me. It was a little selfish for me to think though, but I wanted to still be involved in finding out who was controlling Morpheus.

And then I would have to decide between this world and Wonderland.

I felt less bitter about this world after Lilith moved out and Kate and I were able to start actually thinking about our future. It used to seem so far away, yet now it was practically around the corner. It was nerve-wracking, to say the least, and kept me up more nights than not.

After all the packets of paper were passed around, Mr. Lewis flipped open his own copy. "Now, the main thing you need to look at is what is due each week. On

Fridays you'll have an open-note quiz over everything I taught during the week. If I notice that more than sixty percent of you failed a question, then I will throw it out. Mondays we will go over the quiz and any questions I feel people didn't understand. Along with that, on Mondays you will also be required to turn in a summary of readings that are meant to help me make sure you understand everything. On top of the textbook, you will have extra readings that will be provided to you on Canvas. There shouldn't be more than fifty pages total to read per week."

The whole class made an audible gasp. That was a lot. Why did he not think that was a lot? It sounded like busywork to me.

"Then the other things you should put in your calendar, which I recommend using to mark all your due dates, are the tests. There will be a midterm and final each semester, with the final in the spring being the practice AP exam. Then you will also have two five-page essays due this semester, along with the field trip essay and one ten-page essay due next semester. The topics are of your choosing, but I must give the okay for them before you turn them in. Start thinking about it now so you can begin working on them as soon as possible."

Mr. Lewis took a look at the other students, whom I expected all appeared as terrified as I did. "This may seem like a lot, but it's to prepare you for college. College classes will have a lot more work than this, so hopefully you all pass the AP exam and are able to get some credits."

Hopefully was the key word there. If I didn't, my parents would be pissed. I sighed as I started flipping through the syllabus some more. Maybe I could write a paper on Lewis Carroll's *Alice's Adventures in Wonderland* and how it related to society…

Morning came and went and luckily pre-calc. didn't seem like it would be too difficult, which was a surprise. Honors English, however, was going to have a lot of busy work just like AP European history. *Alice's Adventures in Wonderland* was on the reading list, so at least I could kind of cheat and read that for credit. I had a feeling the teacher was going to argue with me on some of my remarks, but I would try to keep my lips shut. After those classes, I had Advanced Art, which was going to be fun. We would be going over oils and watercolors and different techniques. It was a nice break in the middle of the day.

Lunch was somewhat normal, other than Malcolm not being there. Chase took a seat next to me, and Melvin and Davis took the seats across from us. Kate, of course, had a track meeting since it was the first day of school. I opened my bento, a little sad now that I only had to make one and didn't have anyone to share it with.

"Floral-themed as always, huh?" Chase asked as he peered inside.

I nodded. "Yeah, they are easy to cut out. If I didn't do floral, I would probably get too geeky and just make anime-themed ones."

"Oh? And what's wrong with that? I like all the manga you have had me read so far. The stories are a blast! A lot more interesting than what we have to read for English class."

He definitely had a point there.

Chase went on. "And you still have your *Sailor Moon* backpack, so I don't think it would be to anyone's surprise. Also, you forget, we are practically invisible at this school. We aren't jocks, we aren't really smart, Malcolm's not here, so there are no girls following us around anymore."

I let out a sigh. "Thanks for reminding me that I don't fit in here."

"You fit in with us though!" Davis commented.

I gave him a small smile. That was kind of the problem—I fit into their world a lot better than this one. I wanted to stay there, but the problem of leaving people behind still was an issue.

Chase made a cut-it-out gesture that I caught in the corner of my eye. He tried not to bring up my having to choose since it always dampened the mood, and he knew it was already on my mind. I would just have to wait and see what happened in Wonderland next.

"I am glad I have you all. It definitely has made the entire high school experience a lot more lively."

"Especially when Kenny was student teaching—that was an entire debacle." Melvin took a bite of his sandwich, shaking his head.

"And don't forget Bill as the PE teacher!" Davis added.

I laughed. That was definitely entertaining. Problem was, no one except us remembered it as Bill and Kenny needed to stay back in Wonderland, so Malcolm erased their existence.

Just like what would happen if I decided to stay in Wonderland.

Everyone remembered Malcolm, however, but everyone was told that he simply moved back home to Colorado. I wasn't sure why he picked Colorado, but it worked. Everyone acted like it answered all the questions they had about his character.

Chase shuttered. "Don't bring up Kenny. I don't want to think about his room right now."

"That bad, huh?" I asked. The Queen and King had ordered Chase to clean Kenny's room for a year due to him disobeying direct orders during the battle against Morpheus. Malcolm, on the other hand, had been ordered to stay in Wonderland and not be allowed to go to Earth unless needed, which he wasn't. Then right after that, we broke up due to him not wanting me to pick Wonderland.

"He has no sense of decency. There are constantly dirty dishes and his clothes are everywhere. I don't even want to know what half the stains are from. It's the worst job I have ever had, and that is saying a lot."

We all laughed. It was nice to still have moments like these, but with Malcolm gone and time running out, I couldn't stop the worry that constantly filled my heart. How long was this going to last?

CHAPTER TWO

I stared at the AP biology syllabus, trying not to cry. This was so much work—there was no way I was going to finish all of it every week and be able to juggle the other classes. My parents expected too much of me—I needed to drop something.

But what? I needed the science credit, and there was no way I would pass general chemistry or physics. This was the only class. And I wasn't going to throw away my chance of going to Europe. I just would have to work really hard.

Chase leaned over and whispered into my ear, "We will get through this. Don't worry. We can study in

Wonderland. It will give us more time."

I slowly nodded. Honestly, we tried studying in Wonderland, but it never seemed to work out. We would always get distracted and nothing got done, or at least for school. Plenty got done for matters in Wonderland. But school never felt important over there.

There was also the fact my seventeenth birthday was in April, before the AP exams in May, so he actually wouldn't be taking it. At least he would be around until then and helping me with labs.

I flipped to the page that outlined the lab reports. I collapsed my head on the desk as Chase patted my back.

Thank goodness there was one consistent thing in my life I could always look forward to—dance class.

I still rode my bike to class and would until it started raining and got cold, so for at least three or four more weeks. I got my sister's old car as she and my parents went halves with a new one for her for college. She was also living close to campus and wouldn't need it that often. Having a car definitely made the summer a lot more fun, as Kate and I could go up to Portland and the beach together. It would have been a lot more fun if Malcolm had still been around, but I tried not to think about it too often.

I locked my bike outside dance and was joined by

Chase, who showed up out of nowhere. Even though I knew I should have been used to him appearing and disappearing randomly, I still let out a quiet yelp.

He laughed. "Every time."

My face turned red. "You know, I change in the bathroom at home now thanks to you, and my sister started questioning why. I had to come up with some lie instead of saying you keep showing up in my room, and I don't want you to catch me changing."

"How else am I going to show up? You don't want your parents to know about me, do you?"

I let out a defeated sigh. He definitely had a point. If my parents found out he and I were hanging out, there would be a lot of drama. It wasn't like we were dating either. Though if they knew sometimes he stayed the night, I don't think I would ever get to leave the house again.

"Hey, I forgot to check before you left, but you didn't forget your dance shoes today, did you?"

I slammed my hand on my face. "Ugh!"

He held out his hand. "Locker or at home?"

"At home this time," I explained as we walked around the warehouse where no one could see. In an instant we were inside my room. I grabbed my dance shoes that were hung on my door, where I thought I wouldn't forget them, but I was clearly wrong and grabbed Chase's hand again. We were back at the studio just like that.

"You definitely come in handy at times like this, Chase," I commented as I laughed. That was definitely close.

He crossed his arms and winked at me. "And you definitely haven't learned your lesson after all this time."

"Clearly not. I don't know what I will do without you."

Chase hesitated. "So you are going to stay here?"

I shook my head. "I don't know yet. I just… It's a hard decision to make, you know?"

He nodded. "Yeah, just take your time, and I will support you either way."

I smiled. "Thanks, Chase." I gave him a hug, then we turned to the studio and went inside.

Trevor, a boy from North High with shaggy black hair and was one of the leads in a lot of our performances, pointed at the two of us. "There's the two lovebirds! I saw you two go back behind the warehouse! What were you two doing? Making out?"

My face had to have turned beet red. I ran to the changing room, as if that would be an escape. It wouldn't be, as I would need to go back out there where everyone would ask questions. I felt a little bad having left Chase out there to fend for himself. Mandy and Sydney, who were also changing, gave me side glances with a smirk.

"So when did you two start dating?" Mandy asked.

I squeezed my eyes shut as if I could will it all away. "It's not like that!"

"Oh?" Sydney leaned against the wall with her arms folded. "Then what were you two doing behind the warehouse?"

What was I going to say? Teleporting back to get my shoes? And what did Chase come up with? My guess was that our stories wouldn't match. I shouldn't have run off.

"There was a cat, and we chased it back there. It was a cute orange one with stripes and everything. It wouldn't let us get near though." It was the best I could come up with. Hopefully they would buy it.

"I guess that would make sense. You two are pretty close though. I wouldn't be surprised if you two had a hidden romance." Sydney slipped on her ballet flats.

I shook my head. "No, we aren't. Sorry to disappoint."

Mandy sighed. "That means I lost the bet. Sad day."

Wait, they were all taking bets on whether or not Chase and I were dating? It felt like my face was even redder. Ugh, when would this day end?

After I'd finished changing, I went out in the main practice area to find the guys all talking to Chase. I prayed his story matched mine. I mean, he was the

Cheshire cat, right? He would come up with a cat story, or at least I hoped.

He turned his head when I came up to him and smiled. "Hey! I cleared it all up. I told them there was a cat and we were following it."

Oh thank God. I smiled. "That's what I said. An orange one, right?"

Chase sort of frowned. "Or black and white. Or both, there was two, right?"

I could see all the dancers around us start to smile as if they had caught our lie.

"Yeah. There was more than one cat…"

Everyone started snickering, and I felt like I wanted to cry. Chase just shrugged. He didn't seem to care.

When would this day just end?

I took a sip of my mint tea as Chase downed his espresso. Today was the longest day in history. First I learned how much work would be needed to pass my classes, and then the entire dance class thought they caught Chase and me making out. I could only deal with so much in one day.

"I don't think you should worry. I doubt it would even matter if they believe we are dating anyway. I mean, it sounded like they already were thinking it."

I let out a defeated sigh. "Yeah, I suppose you are right."

"I mean, it's not like it's a bad thing. They may tease, but they always have."

He stared at me as if waiting for a response. What was that about?

I took a sip of my tea. "I guess it won't change things. It's not like they would understand the truth anyway."

"Right, so let's just forget about it, I guess."

I nodded. I didn't think I could take silly drama like that on top of schoolwork and dance and art and Wonderland. I would just have to ignore it until it went away. If I didn't respond to their teasing, then they would stop. It wasn't like they were actually bullying but more were just making accusations.

"So what class are you looking forward to the most?" I asked, wanting to forget about my worries even if school was one of them.

"I think woodshop is going to be fun."

"Yeah! Me too! I'm glad you decided to take it with me. I can't believe I have two art classes and a study hall, yet I still feel like the rest of the work is going to be overwhelming. Heck, even shop and art is going to be a lot of time. People act like those types of classes are easy, but really it's a different set of skills one needs to master."

"Definitely. But I think the two of us will manage."

I shrugged and looked down at my drink. "Hopefully.

I mean, next semester it won't really matter for you since you will have to leave…"

Chase and I were quiet for a moment, then he downed the rest of his drink. "You could come with. Then you won't have to stress so much, at least not about school."

I fidgeted with my dress a little. "But what about my family? And Kate?"

"What about Wonderland? What about Kenny? And Davis? They are probably going to start crying if you decided to stay here."

I let out a brief laugh even though I felt like tearing up. He was right. They probably would start crying, but would they beg me to stay? If Malcolm was around, probably not as he doesn't want me to choose Wonderland. For some reason he didn't want me to stay even though he loved me… or at least used to love me.

"And…," Chase went on. "I would be pretty bummed if you left us."

I grabbed his hand and squeezed it a little. "Thanks."

We sat like that for a few moments, holding hands in silence, but eventually Chase pulled his hand away. "We should go check in with Wonderland this weekend. Last I heard was that there was some progress being made on figuring out the true identity of Morpheus. It was a good thing that he revealed what he was to you, or we wouldn't have had anything to start with."

I nodded. "Yeah, good thing." Memories of Malcolm cutting off Morpheus's head came rushing back to me. I had found out Malcolm's true role in Wonderland during the first Alice's visit—he was the executioner of Wonderland. I knew that it was all in the past, and he couldn't disobey his role back then, but after seeing what he did to Morpheus, and so easily… It made me a little afraid, and I wondered if I truly did know him.

But at the same time, it had been so many years ago.

Chase went on. "So I was thinking Friday night after your parents went to bed, we could head over? Then we could get all caught up, perhaps help with some stuff and be back by morning. And have the rest of the weekend to go through all the homework we have for the semester. Maybe head to the library to meet up or something. Or a café."

I nodded. "Yeah, that sounds good. Will you be coming by tonight?"

He shrugged. "I mean, if you want me to. It's not like Morpheus is around, and you were just saying how you don't like me randomly appearing and all that."

I poked my fingers together. "Yeah, but I was able to pick up this new manga I haven't read yet, and I wanted to share it with you. It's called *Seraph of End*, and it has vampires and sounds really cool."

He laughed. "Fine. I guess I can come by. It will be a nice end to a long day."

I smiled. "Exactly."

CHAPTER THREE

The week went by, and I was able to finish most of the homework and readings. Kate helped a lot after school, and I tried to figure out a schedule where I would be able to manage it all. Once midterms came around, I didn't know what I was going to do. I would probably end up crying to Kate on each test, before and after. The two of us would have to plan to study together.

I checked the clock, and it was almost ten at night, and my parents were going to bed for the night. I put on one of my floral sundresses and waited for Chase to appear. I made sure one of my anime body pillows was tucked in nicely, in case my parents peeked in my bedroom in the middle of the night.

After a few more minutes of waiting, I saw my parents' light turn off from under their door. I quietly closed my own door and turned around to find Chase there. I was able to hold back a scream this time.

"What did I say about doing that?" I whispered.

He shrugged. "Well, what else was I going to do? Knock? Besides, you knew I was coming."

He had a fair point. I folded my arms. "Whatever, let's get on with it."

Chase grinned as he wrapped his arms around me. "Here we go, Alice."

We fell back through the closet doorway and we fell down… and down… and down…

I didn't understand why we always had to fall like this. I was getting better at not feeling sick at least, but my stomach still turned a bit.

We finally hit the soft grass, and I found myself half on Chase and half on the ground.

"Oof!"

"Sorry about that, Chase… Although it's your fault since you pull me back through the door."

"True. Just can you get up? It's dark and I don't want to reach out and pull an anime cliché."

I laughed a little as I stood up, careful not to hit the

pipe I knew was above me. I had hit my head enough times to be wary of it now. Chase also got up and went to open the door. It was daylight in Wonderland, which I was glad for as I wasn't that sleepy.

He looked back at me, his hair now purple with cat ears on the top of his head. "Ready Alice?"

I nodded as I grabbed his shoulder, and he transported us into the castle. Moments later I found myself in the middle of the palace.

And five seconds later, there were swords pointed at our faces.

"Chase! How many times have I told you not to transport straight into the palace?" Bill came running down the hallway. "You are supposed to check in at the front so we know you are here."

"But this is faster. Besides, it's payback for cleaning Kenny's room. You have a disgusting boyfriend."

Bill cocked a grin. "I know."

I clapped my hands together to stop this awkward conversation. "So I heard you all found something of interest?"

Bill nodded. "Yes. Come this way."

We followed Bill toward one of the meeting rooms. Melvin, Malcolm, and Davis were already in the room at a table, going through stacks of papers. The moment I walked in, Malcolm looked up at me. We exchanged glances and then both looked away. I was glad to see we were both awkward, as always.

"So," Chase began as he saw Malcolm and I try to ignore each other. "What do you have for us?"

Melvin pulled out a folder from one of the piles. "We were able to figure out the identity of a handful of the people that make up Morpheus. We still aren't done and want a little help narrowing down the rest. We think they all had some things in common but haven't quite figured out what those are. Once we do that, we can go to the locations they once lived at and see if we can find out anything. There could be letters or something that had been left behind."

"You think there would be letters?" I asked as I took a seat. "I would think he would have burned them to make sure he didn't get caught."

"There could be evidence or a piece in the fireplaces. We will make sure to sweep the area. But first we need to narrow it down. We have at least a hundred more potential files to work through, and then we will be set."

A hundred? That didn't sound like just a few. How many had they gone through since the spring if there were still that many left? "What should we look for?"

Bill shrugged. "Anything noteworthy and anything you see that might link quite a few. We aren't sure how many dreams combined to Morpheus, but if I had to guess, it was at least five, if not ten."

I nodded. That made the most sense after everything he had explained. "And what are these files?"

Malcolm actually answered. "These are all files of people who disappeared before or while Morpheus was known. It is just a fraction of what was discovered. Most, of course, were killed by him from his power with the circus."

A fraction of those killed by everything that happened. He was a monster, thinking that he was doing good. But of course this monster had an owner, and we needed to figure out who it was that had actually been pulling the strings.

"Okay, where do you want me to start?"

Hours had gone by before we finished combing through the files they had left. None of us found anything. Bill and Malcolm had said these were the only people to go missing right before the circus. They had to question many citizens and try to figure out the dates of each death, as time did weird things in this world. Some of those people could have simply died from whatever happened to the person they were connected with in my world. I felt bad, but I wasn't the one who created this world and the ties it had.

I set down the last file and rubbed my eyes. "What time is it?"

"It's almost time for dinner. I think we should call it a

day." Bill leaned back in his chair and stretched. "We can go through all these files again in the morning."

Malcolm stood up and didn't say anything as he went to the door, leaving us. He clearly didn't want to eat dinner together. I turned away from the door, pain forming in my chest. Why did things have to be this way between us? Why couldn't we go back to being friends like we were when I'd first come to Wonderland?

Were we ever just friends though? I always had a crush on him before I found out about Wonderland, and it seemed like Malcolm always had an interest in me, whether it was because he had feelings for me or because he and the other Alice were once a couple. Either way, it was all messed up now, and I didn't know if we could ever fix it.

"Hey, Alice." Chase jumped up from the spot he had been sitting on the floor and made his way toward me. "I heard there is a new shop in the district that serves ramen. They say it is really good."

I looked up at him, his catlike eyes watching me closely. I could see his violet tail swaying back and forth behind him. At first it was so strange to see him like a cat, but I got used to it. Perhaps it was because of all the anime and manga I consumed.

I smiled. "Yeah, that sounds good."

Melvin and Davis stood up. Davis squeaked. "Can I

join?"

"Ramen does sound good… Could I come as well?" Melvin asked as he ruffled his rabbit ears. I really wanted to touch them again but didn't as he really hated it. They were so fluffy though.

I nodded. "Of course."

Bill yawned. "I think I am going to call it a day and retire. Kenny probably has tarts or something waiting for me. You kids have fun."

Chase led us out of the palace and toward the new ramen shop. As we stepped outside, I found that the sky was already dark and stars filled the sky. Technically I had been awake far past my bedtime, but when I was in Wonderland, I never noticed. I wasn't sure if that was because I was used to pulling all-nighters, because Wonderland affected my energy levels, or because I was full of adrenaline while I was here, but I definitely was beginning to feel tired. Once I had a belly full of ramen, I would probably pass out.

The ramen shop wasn't too far from the castle and was one of the busiest shops around. It must have just opened as the line went out the door. I feared it would be hours before we would be able to get a seat, like Olive Garden on Lancaster, and frowned a little.

Chase laughed. "Don't worry, Alice, there is always a seat open for those who work in the castle at all the shops. Let me just talk to the hostess."

He disappeared for a moment, then came back with a smile. "We have a table. Follow me."

Melvin, Davis, and I followed him inside the crowded restaurant, and we were able to get a table in the back. Chase pulled out the chair for me.

"Thanks." I sat down and took a look at the menu. The house special ramen, with a creamy broth, pork, corn, and bok choy, sounded appetizing. The vegetarian option sounded good as well, but I was craving protein. There was also an option to add an egg, which I knew I would do. Eggs in ramen were always the best.

"Are you ready?" Chase asked.

I nodded. "Yeah, as long as the others are ready."

Melvin set the menu down. "After centuries of being alive, we know what we like."

Davis nodded. "Yup, pretty much."

We each ordered our dinner, and Chase ordered a couple of servings of edamame as an appetizer. The waitress left, and we awaited our food.

"See, this world has everything you love," Chase commented. "There isn't anything you can't have."

"Chase…," Melvin began.

"What? It's not like Malcolm is here to yell at me for bringing it up. Besides, she knows she has to make a choice."

I ignored the question. I didn't want to think about it any longer and wanted to just enjoy my meal. The fact the others didn't want to bring it up because of Malcolm made my chest hurt even worse. Why didn't he want me to stay? Why was he being like this? Was it because sometime in the future another Alice would come to save Wonderland and I would be replaced? He loved the first Alice, so would it forever be the same? Or did he just realize I couldn't replace her and that was why he didn't want me around any longer?

"Alice, are you okay?" Chase asked.

I pushed back all the thoughts and forced a smile. "Yeah, I'm fine."

"See, Chase, you need to stop bringing it up." Davis kicked Chase in the leg under the table.

"Ow. Whatever. But it's something that needs to be addressed sooner rather than later. Going on like it's not an issue is stupid."

He had a point. I was going to say how much I did like it here, but the waitress came back with the ramen bowls. As I was about to tell her thank you, I noticed something on her face. It was a mole, which really didn't stand out to me normally, but after looking at pictures for hours, I realized what the connection was.

"I figured it out!" I shouted, almost causing the waitress to dump Chase's ramen all over him.

CHAPTER FOUR

We all met back at the meeting room. Poor Bill looked like he had already fallen asleep. I wanted to go to sleep as well, but I knew I would forget what I noticed.

"What did you figure out, Alice?" He yawned. He didn't even bother changing back into his suit but wore his pajama pants and shirt. The shirt had a giant ace on it, and the pants were covered in card suits. It made me smile a little.

I pulled together a few of the profiles that we had gone through earlier that day and pointed at the faces.

"It's the mole. Morpheus had a faint mole on his cheek. I never gave it much thought, but a good chunk of these people that went missing all had moles on their cheeks. I think it might be the connection. It occurred to me when I saw our waitress and she had a mole on her chin."

Bill flipped through the files I had found. "This could be a start. We can meet back up in the morning and figure out where all the ones who have moles on their faces live and start searching."

"Way to go, Alice!" Chase patted my back. I smiled, glad I was able to help. As I glanced at Malcolm, I found him glaring at Chase. Did he not like how close Chase and I were as friends now? It wasn't like things had changed between Chase and me, as we always had been friends, but it seemed to bother Malcolm.

"Good job," Malcolm said as he gathered the files. "I will go ahead and get some of the work done and ready it for the morning. You all go get some rest."

I hesitated. "But don't you need some rest?"

Malcolm shook his head. "I'm not tired. You all go ahead. I presume you have had a long day."

"Okay, thanks…" I started for the door when Chase called after me.

"Wait up! I'll walk you to your room."

I turned and found Chase hurrying after me. Behind him, Malcolm tried not to glare at Chase more, but failed miserably. It made me a little happy he was jealous Chase was walking with me, but I immediately felt guilty about that. They used to fight about me all the time, even when we were dating. Malcolm was the one who agreed to break it off, so he shouldn't still get jealous about Chase. Either way, I would definitely leave that fight between the two of them, as I did not need more drama in my life.

The door to the meeting room closed behind us, and I let out a breath.

"What is it?" Chase asked.

I shook my head. "It's nothing. Anyway, do you think once we search these guys' homes, we will find anything? I mean, it seems like it has been a while since they disappeared. Wouldn't someone else buy the house or take over it?"

Chase shrugged. "Not necessarily. The people in Wonderland are still trying to get their lives back together after Morpheus, so most of those homes are still abandoned and untouched."

He made a fair point. It was like after a war when everything was still untouched, but in this case nothing was in ruins, except the old Kingdoms of course.

"Then tomorrow will be interesting for sure. Hopefully we find something. Then we can get to the bottom of it all."

Nodding, he looked away a little. "Yeah, hopefully."

The only problem was, once we solved this mystery, I would either have to choose Wonderland or go back home forever. I tried to look at the bright side of it all—at least Wonderland would finally be safe and we wouldn't have to worry about whoever was behind it trying something else. Sure, someone in the future might try to attack, but that would be a long time from now. And I would either still be here or I would be long gone.

I guess that really wasn't a bright side.

"And then we will have a bunch of homework to finish up." I laughed.

Chase shook his head. "There is so much homework this year. It's kind of ridiculous."

"My parents are going to kill me if I don't keep up my grades. I mean, they forced me to take the AP classes so I can get a head start for college. They still don't want me to go to a specialized school, but we will see."

"Your world is so much more complicated than ours."

I shrugged. "I… guess? I think it is just different. There are some pretty complicated things in this world as well. But now that I think about it, you might be right. My world makes things a lot more complicated than they need to be and prioritizes the wrong things."

We ventured down farther through the hallway and

came upon my room. It always felt weird having my own room in Wonderland, and in a palace nonetheless. I would miss it if I didn't stay there.

I turned to Chase. "Well, I guess I will see you in the morning, Chase. Come get me when everyone is ready to meet up."

He nodded. "I will. Don't you worry about that."

"Good night."

He hesitated. "Good night, Alice."

I entered my room to find it just as it normally appeared. This place felt like home for me even if it wasn't filled with art and anime. I sighed as I changed out of my dress and into the pajamas I kept here and hugged my stuffed giraffe.

Hopefully we would find something about this mastermind soon, or I felt like I wasn't any help to Wonderland any longer.

I woke up to someone knocking at my door.

"Alice, time to get up!" Chase called out from the other side of the door. Was it morning already?

"Just a minute…" I moaned as I rolled out of bed. Why did mornings always suck, no matter where I was? I needed a cup of tea, stat.

I changed into my typical button-up shirt and trousers that worked perfectly for exploring Wonderland. I brushed my hair with my fingers and hoped for the best as I opened the door.

"Hey!" Chase smiled at me, his tail wagging back and forth behind him.

I rolled my eyes at him. "Why are you always so hyper in the morning?"

He spread out his arms. "Because the whole day is ahead of us! Anything is possible!"

"And you already had an espresso?"

"And I already had an espresso!" He grinned widely.

That sounded about right. It was like giving catnip to a kitten. He was hyper and could run around for hours. Literally.

I closed the door behind me, and we started down the hallway. "Where are the others?"

"They are grabbing breakfast and are going to meet us in the room. I think Davis is grabbing you something. You like cheese, right?" He joked.

"Better than tuna," I retorted.

"If you are awake enough for a comment like that, I think you don't need the caffeine."

"You never need caffeine, and yet you are always drinking some, so I don't think you have room to talk Chase."

"Fair."

We headed back toward the meeting room to find Bill stacking all the files and Kenny with his face in a corner.

"Uh, what happened this time?" I asked as I took a seat.

"Bill said I'm not allowed to touch any more files because I dropped a few. So I'm standing here so I don't cause trouble."

"Not just a few," Bill commented. "You dropped all of them, making Malcolm angry and go out for a walk. You know how bad you have to make him in order for him to walk off like that?"

Kenny murmured, "How was I supposed to know he was in a foul mood?"

"He's been in a foul mood for a while." Bill glanced over at me. "So just assume it for the time being."

I didn't comment, and we sat there in silence. It wasn't my problem he wasn't over the breakup, as he was the one who caused it. I felt a little responsible though. Chase took a seat next to me, and we waited until Melvin and Davis showed up a few moments later.

"Alice, I got you some tea and a bagel with cream cheese."

Chase and I started laughing. Davis's face went flush.

"Just because I am a mouse doesn't mean that's why I got cream cheese! Most people put cream cheese on bagels!"

I held back the rest of my laughs. "Thank you, Davis. You are right. I'm sorry."

I took a bite of the bagel and was immediately

pleased. The bagels in Wonderland were the best I ever had. This one had strawberries and blueberries in it and tasted a little like vanilla. I wished I could eat these every morning.

Taking a sip of the tea, I found the flavors to be quite spectacular as well. "What kind of tea is this, Davis?"

"It's peach-hibiscus black tea. It sounded good, so I thought you would like it."

I nodded. "It's great. Thanks."

We ate the rest of our meal and waited for Malcolm to come back around. As Davis and I took the last bite, as apparently we were the slowest eaters there, Malcolm came back inside and took a seat across from me next to Bill.

"Now that we are all here"—Bill glanced at Malcolm and Kenny, who was now allowed back at the table —"we can discuss the next step."

Malcolm unrolled a map. "We believe the individuals who combined to form Morpheus each resided in a different district. We will split up into teams of two to check out the houses. Each group will be searching two or three homes, and we will meet back here after."

I raised my hand. "May I go to the flower district? I wanted to stop by the farmer who brought me here to give them a painting I have in my room. I've been meaning to do it for a while but just haven't had time."

Malcolm nodded. "Yeah, that will work."

Chase wrapped his arm around me. "Alice and I will be a team."

Malcolm tapped his fingers on the table. "Fine. Melvin and Davis will be a team. Bill and the White Rabbit will be a team, wherever he is. I assume he is with the King and Queen. Drag him outside; he needs to get fresh air more often. And Kenny, you will be with me."

Kenny frowned. "But I want to be with Bill."

"But you two never get anything done."

He nodded. "That's fair. I'm excited to journey with you, Malcolm. I bet we will have loads of fun."

Malcolm stared at Kenny for a moment, as if debating on changing his groups. "Yeah, whatever. Here are the locations of the homes of the missing people." He handed out two or three folders to each of us. "Everyone stay safe and make sure you are armed. You never know what may happen."

Chase grabbed the folders and flipped through them. "Seems easy enough. I bet you and I will be the first ones done, Alice."

"Because you can teleport. That's why you will be searching three locations," Malcolm commented. "And don't slack off."

Chase gave Malcolm a look. "What's that supposed to mean, Mad Hatter?"

They held each other's gaze for a moment when I

finally stood up. "Right, let's get going, Chase."

He smirked and gave Malcolm a triumphant look. "Right, let's."

CHAPTER FIVE

"Wow, Alice, that's a beautiful painting," Chase commented as we went back to my room to grab the gift for Penny and her husband.

I smiled. "Thank you. I worked really hard on it. I think it might be one of the best paintings I've ever done."

"And you are still willing to give it away?" he asked. "If you feel it's your best, are you okay with parting with it?"

"Of course. I believe art is for sharing, not for

hoarding. Hopefully they like it."

"I think they will."

I double-checked the room to make sure I wasn't missing anything. Chase waited for me to finish and then commented, "Well, are you ready?"

"Yup! But according to Bill, we will have to teleport outside the castle, just in case."

He let out a sigh. "Fine, whatever. They are way overcautious."

"Yeah, says the guy who let Bill find the hideout and capture me."

Chase rolled his eyes. "That was so long ago, okay? And we don't have to worry about people after us."

"Except the person who is behind Morpheus."

"Yeah, but if they were going to attack, they would have by now. It won't have anything to do with me teleporting."

"Fair, but unless you want to clean Kenny's room for even longer, I would follow orders."

"Fine. I will obey their rule just this once."

We laughed as we went into the hallway and headed toward the entrance to the palace. As we made our way through the maze, we ran into a familiar face.

"Crap," Chase whispered under his breath.

I put on my best smile. It wasn't that I hated the Duchess, but I didn't care to talk to her. She acted like the perfect French Lolita character, and it could be a bit much for me. And I knew she would talk forever, and we had work to do.

"Alice! I see that you are back in Wonderland." She kissed each of my cheeks.

"Yup. We are about to go out for a mission, so we better hurry."

"Oh, to look for the person behind Morpheus?" she asked with a bit of a surprised look. "Did you find any leads?"

Chase and I glanced at each other. Most of what we were doing was secret, although rumors about there being a mastermind had gotten around.

"We are still working on it," I commented. "Whatever is going on is quite complex."

She grabbed my hands. "Well, Alice, I just know you will find them. Especially since you have my loyal little kitty cat with you. He is the strongest person I know and quite clever when he isn't causing trouble. Just stop whoever is behind this before it is too late. Time is ticking, Alice."

I wasn't sure what she meant by that—if she just meant time in general or about how I would have to pick between Wonderland and my world.

"Thank you, Duchess. We will see you later."

She did a curtsy, and I did the same out of habit from dance. It felt weird to do without a dress or costume on, but I didn't pay much mind as the Duchess went on with her little walk.

Chase let out a sigh. "Why did she have to show up to kill the mood? She is so good at doing that, you know."

"I don't think she is all bad—just a bit much."

"Yeah, easy for you to say." He glanced back at her with a little bit of worry in his eyes. "Whatever. We better get to the front of the palace."

Chase and I hurried outside before anyone else could stop us, not that there were many who would want to talk with us. For the most part, it was only those who had roles that gave us much mind. Otherwise, we were mainly ignored by the dreams. I liked getting to know some of the dreams, however, as all of them had such interesting lives, such as Penny and Zachariah.

Chase grabbed my hand. "Ready?"

I nodded, and poof we were in the Garden District. I stared around in awe, as the Garden District had buildings that were covered in vegetation. Flowers of all types and colors bloomed bright in the sun. Even the walkways were made of grass and moss—and most people didn't even wear shoes. The atmosphere felt pleasant, and everyone was smiling.

Maybe that was what we were missing in my world —we needed to be more connected to nature like this.

I glanced around at all the people's smiling faces. I could spend days here, drawing and painting scenery with people going about their day. Perhaps I would get a chance once we found whoever was behind this.

Turning to Chase, I smiled. "It sure is handy that you can transport us here so fast."

He bowed a little. "A cat's pleasure. We can go anywhere whenever you want, Alice. Just say the word."

Glancing around, I pointed toward a hill. "I believe the house is out that way. Can you transport us over there?"

"As you wish." Chase transferred us to the top of the hill. I scanned the floral fields. Now that we were back here during the day, I saw the splendor of all the wildflowers that grew across the land. There were violets, bluebells, carnations, sunflowers, poppies, hydrangeas, and many others. I definitely would need to bring my art supplies here one day. And these flowers were much more beautiful than those in the Dark Forest, as they didn't sing a deadly song. But I did want to paint those someday as well.

I pointed at a small farm in the distance with a white house in the middle. "That one."

Chase nodded, and in a moment, we appeared at their door. I was a little taken aback, as I figured he would transport us away from the house.

I turned to him. "You know, I would have teleported us a bit away so they could see us coming?"

Chase grinned. "It's more fun to scare people."

"I've noticed you enjoy that." I knocked on the door. A few moments later, a woman, whom I remembered was named Penny, opened the door.

"Alice! What are you doing here? I didn't see you come down the road. Please come in."

I gave Chase a look as we stepped into the small two-story home. Katherine, Penny's daughter who was probably around seven years old, came running when she saw me, her brown curls dancing all around.

"Alice!" she yelled as she wrapped her arms around me. "You came back!"

I knelt down to her level. "I did. And you have grown so much!"

"She has," Penny commented. "Now, would you two like a pot of wildflower tea? I was just about to put the kettle on."

"If it isn't a hassle, I would love to try it," I said as I held out the painting. "And this is for you. I painted it myself."

Penny's eyes widened. "This is beautiful, Alice. You are an amazing artist. Zachariah will love it."

"Thank you. It is the least I could do since you two helped me get back to the palace. I wanted to show my thanks."

Penny set the painting down on the table and gestured to the seats. "Please, take a seat while the tea brews."

Chase and I took a seat as Katherine crowded her mother. Chase leaned over to whisper in my ear, "Alice, we need to hurry and search the other houses."

"Yes, but one of them is nearby. Maybe she knows something about it."

Chase leaned back. "Fair enough. We can ask. But if we get in trouble for being late, you are the one who is going to get in trouble."

"I will take full responsibility. I promise."

Penny brought out the tea after a few moments and took a seat herself. "So what brings you out to these parts?"

I blew on the tea. "We were actually looking into a disappearance around here. Does the name Denis Lavendor sound familiar to you?"

Penny took a sip of her tea. "Actually, it does."

"Can you tell us more?" Chase asked.

She bit her lip. "He was a really nice guy. He used to come over for dinner with his family. We would make a pot roast and talk about the harvest."

"Family?" I asked. "What happened to them?"

Penny shrugged as she nursed her cup. "We really don't know. They actually all disappeared at the same time."

"His whole family?" Chase asked. "Did the authorities ever find out what happened?"

"No, they didn't. They just seemed to vanish, and they weren't able to find any trace. They figured they ran off. Usually when there're bodies, they can tell if it is natural or not… but in this case they had completely vanished."

Chase shook his head. "But no one can just run away… and back then no one was threatening them."

"We never understood either. But we went out to check up on them one day, and they were gone. No one in the community saw them leave, and since then, no one has gone in their house. They say it is haunted."

"Why haunted?" I gulped. I wasn't one for haunted houses, even the fake ones.

"Sometimes we see lights turn on and off and figures around the house, but every time someone goes to check it out, there's no one there and the lights are off."

Chase and I glanced at each other. "Well…," he began. "At least we aren't going in the dark."

I rolled my eyes as I took a sip of my tea. It was floral and sweet. I didn't know what flowers she included in it, but the taste was beautiful.

"If you do find anything out about what happened, please let us know so we can tell the community. There were so many unanswered questions, and many of us fear it could happen again."

I couldn't imagine what all these people had gone through in the past couple of years. They had lost a lot of friends and then went through the whole circus ordeal and almost died. Then Morpheus was on the loose and they were all afraid. Now they had to deal with the possibility of someone else trying to take over Wonderland.

"We will let you know what we find," I said. Chase glanced at me with his cat eyes but didn't say anything. I finished up my drink. "Thank you so much for the tea. It is lovely."

"You are welcome here at any time. Zachariah is going to love the painting."

Chase and I stood up and started for the door. Katherine hugged me one more time as we stepped outside. "I am going to miss you."

"I will miss you too. I promise I will stop by later, okay?"

She nodded and went back to her mom's side. Chase and I waved goodbye to them as we started in the direction of the abandoned house. We walked this time since it was close by.

"They are a good bunch of people," I commented. "I wish more people were like them in my world."

He shrugged. "Trust like that could lead to problems though. If they open their house to the wrong person, they could lose everything."

"It sounds like you are speaking from experience," I commented. "Do you want to talk about it?"

Chase shook his head. "No, not really. It's a long story, and it is in the past now. Don't worry about it."

I nodded. "All right, if you say so. But I'm always here if you need to talk."

He smiled a little. "Thank you, Alice. That means a lot."

We set out toward the abandoned house, hoping to find a clue on who was behind Morpheus and what exactly happened to the family.

CHAPTER SIX

"So this is it?" I asked as we stepped up to the house. It appeared similar to the farmhouses nearby, including Zachariah and Penny's, but something about it screamed "haunted." Perhaps it was the lack of love and life and the fact a few windows were broken and the paint was chipping. Even the field around it was overgrown with wildflowers, which was quite beautiful, but one could tell the difference between a well-kept field and flowers that had taken over the land.

Chase nodded. "Seems to be."

I stared at the front door that was ajar, as if it were asking me to come inside. I was glad it wasn't nighttime as this could easily pass for a haunted house. I could see why there were rumors that ghosts had been spotted. And I wondered if they were true.

I gulped. "Should we look inside?"

"There's nothing to be scared of, Alice. There are no such things as ghosts in Wonderland. I would know."

I turned to him, still not certain. "Then what did the farmers see?"

Chase shrugged. "Perhaps their eyes were playing tricks on them, or…"

"Or what?"

"Or whoever is behind this came back to destroy the evidence."

We stared at each other for a moment, worried that the clues we would be looking for had already been demolished. However, if this was Morpheus's main home, it was possible we would still find something and figure out what happened to his family.

"You first…," I whispered.

Chase rolled his catlike eyes and pushed the door open. It creaked, the sound echoing throughout the house, which made everything much eerier. I really hated this part of our journey and wished we could go back to the palace already.

"Hello?" I called out to the empty home.

Chase gave me a look. "You think someone is here?"

"No, but never hurts to check."

There, of course, was no response. We stepped farther into the house. Dust, dirt, and moss covered most of the space. It smelled stale and a bit like soil.

"Well, at least it will be easy for us to find where the person was looking for evidence." Chase started to carefully look around.

"Oh? What do you mean?"

He gestured around. "All this dust and whatnot. If someone was in here and moving stuff around, we will see a disturbance in it."

I widened my eyes. "That's smart. I would have never thought of that."

Chase grinned. "Yeah, well, I am an expert hunter and all that."

"Because you're a cat?"

"Yup!"

We started searching around the living room first, together of course. There was no way I was going to split up in this house—not when that was how all the horror movies began. And *Scooby Doo*. No, there was safety in numbers.

As we searched, I heard a squeaking sound. Chase's eyes flashed over to where a mouse scurried across the room.

I giggled. "Are you going to catch that and eat it like a cat too?"

"Ew, no. But if Davis were here, I would have caught

it and teased him with it."

"That's so mean."

Chase shrugged. "He could just man up and make me stop. He used to be as feared as Malcolm, as he and Melvin were also executioners, but for some reason the two of them mellowed out enough where everyone forgot that."

That was a strange thought to ponder on. Melvin and Davis shared the same role as Malcolm? They were completely different now, and yet Malcolm was still called "the Mad Hatter" in a derogatory way.

"Granted, Malcolm returned to the forest and they didn't. It took him a long time to get rid of those demons," Chase added.

"I thought you all said he was exiled out there, but now it is sounding like it was his job."

"It was both. He was exiled out there to perform his job. The Queen of Hearts never made sense, to be honest."

"And the Duchess?" I asked as I looked through a bookcase. "Did she make sense?"

Chase frowned. "She's just selfish. I hate her for all the things she had me do."

His eyes turned sad, and I felt a bit bad that I brought it up. "I'm sorry I brought her up... There is still a lot I don't know about Wonderland, and I am just trying to piece together the story versus what really happened."

He shook his head. "It's fine. It was the past. Now we just need to find whatever it is we are looking for."

I nodded as we searched around the living area a little more. A divot in the moss on the ground caught my eye. I pointed at it.

"Doesn't that piece of moss look like it has been picked up and replaced?" I asked.

Chase knelt down. "That it does." He pulled out a knife and carefully lifted it. Underneath there was a broken piece of wood, as if the floorboard had been picked up.

"Appears to be a hiding place." I knelt down next to Chase to get a better look.

"Yeah, but there is nothing in here. It was either cleared out before they disappeared or the figure the neighbors saw took it."

I frowned as we both stood back up.

"Don't worry, Alice. There might be more clues. We just began."

I nodded as we finished inspecting the living room. Although many were faded, pictures of the family hung on the walls. I stared at one that depicted a man with his wife and son. They appeared happy.

"What do you think happened to his family?"

Chase shrugged. "They probably left with him."

"But that doesn't answer the question. I mean, if they had gone with him, wouldn't we have seen them at the circus?"

"Morpheus didn't appear as any of the dreams that made him—maybe the same could be said about his wife and son."

I shook my head. "No, he said he was the only one able to combine like he did."

"Maybe he tried to do the same with his family and it didn't work and they passed."

That was definitely possible, and the thought made me sick to my stomach. Would he have put his wife and son through that? Although it would explain where they went to, I couldn't see Morpheus doing that.

We ventured into the kitchen and dining room, but nothing seemed to stand out, other than they had a fascinating amount of tea cozies. They were all beautifully colored, with most designed as flowers. The more I went through this home, the larger the sinking feeling in my stomach became.

Something horrible happened here if this was indeed Morpheus's true self.

"Should we check upstairs now?" I asked, wrapping my arms around myself. I didn't like being in this happy kitchen any longer, but I doubted I would feel better upstairs.

"Yeah, let's."

There were three bedrooms upstairs. I took a deep breath, preparing myself to look through these rooms.

"Where should we start?" I asked.

Chase nodded to the master bedroom. "Probably his room first. It's possible he hid something in the other rooms but less likely if he didn't know what was really going on."

We entered the master bedroom, and like everything else in this house, it appeared untouched. We scanned around, looking for any signs of disturbance. There didn't seem to be anything moved.

"Maybe someone kept a diary or something." I opened up the drawers on one side of the bed, and Chase checked the other side. I flipped through the books and moved around some of the tincture bottles. I didn't see a diary anywhere.

"Find anything?" I asked.

Chase shook his head. "Nope."

I sat down on the bed and felt something off about the bed. I stood back up and checked under the mattress. It was a diary.

"Bingo!" I flipped through the pages to find what appeared to be a man's handwriting.

Chase came up next to me and peeked over my shoulder. "That definitely looks like a diary. Funny that the person didn't check the most obvious place ever."

"Probably starting near the end would be the best?" I questioned.

"Makes sense to me."

I turned to the last few entries and scanned the notes. I held my hand to mouth.

"Oh my God…"

"What?" Chase asked. I handed it to him to read.

"I write this with tears in my eyes. My son and my lovely wife are dead, taken away from this life due to the actions of the humans in another world." Chase bit his lip. "They have come to me with information that could turn Wonderland upside down. I would be able to live forever and disconnect Wonderland from the human world. All I would have to do is cause destruction so the next Alice will appear."

Everything he did was to bring me to this world. He knew I would come, and that was the plan. This all had been a setup. "Does it say who 'they' are?"

He shook his head. "No. It just goes on saying he left this here because he wanted to leave his life behind. He also kept all the letters from the mastermind in that hidden spot downstairs. And he buried his family out back after they passed away."

I felt bad for the guy. He had lost everything and blamed my world for it. I couldn't blame him—I would have wanted destruction as well.

"The diary might give us more info when we examine it closer. Let's go check the other rooms and then to the other houses just in case there is more to the story."

Chase nodded as he closed the diary and put it in his pocket. We went into the next room, which was the boys' room. It was decorated with ships, almost like it was pirate-themed. I held back the tears I felt for Morpheus going through all this.

There was nothing suspicious or out of the ordinary in the room, and once we were finished, we opened up the third room. Inside the walls were painted a soft pink, and there lay a crib in the middle of the room. Chase pulled out the diary and flipped through the pages.

"They were expecting a girl it looks like."

Chase wrapped his arms around me as I felt tears start to fall down my face. This was incredibly sad, as whatever happened wasn't a singularity—it was something that happened across the districts. Any of these dreams could die at any moment because the people in this world had given up on them.

After a few moments, I backed away. "Sorry about that."

"No worries. Now let's go check out the other houses."

I nodded. "Okay." As we turned to leave, something on the ground that hadn't been there caught my eye. I bent down and grabbed it.

"What's that?" Chase asked.

I unfolded it. It was a letter. "This… this is a letter

from whoever was contacting Morpheus. It must have fallen out of the diary."

Chase's eyes widened. "Really? Let me see that." He took it from my hands and scanned it. "It seems they didn't say who it was."

"But we will be able to look through handwriting samples at the palace, yes? We might be able to narrow it down."

He nodded slowly. "Yeah, this is great news."

I beamed. "Malcolm is going to be really impressed with us."

Chase's eyes glanced into mine. "You still have feelings for him, don't you?"

I turned away. "It's not that simple. I mean… I do, but I don't think he would ever want to be a couple again since he doesn't want me to stay. I mean, I get it, but it still hurts and I don't know if I can trust him if he isn't willing to let me choose."

"Well, I think you should stay. You belong here."

I smiled. "We will see. But first let's finish up for the day."

Chase nodded, and we headed outside and pulled out the file to see which district we would travel to next. In an instant, Chase transported us to the District of Forests.

CHAPTER SEVEN

We didn't find anything of importance in the other two houses in the Forest District. We assumed that although there was a chance they had combined with Morpheus, they weren't contacted by whoever was pulling the strings. I had to admit though, the Forest District was rather cool. It reminded me a little bit of the moon of Endor in *Star Wars, Episode VI*. I expected Ewoks to show up, but they never did. I supposed they were scarier than they actually appeared, so I really wouldn't want to be around one anyway.

The trees in the area were large, and most of the people lived up in them. It was like a village of tree houses. I wanted to draw it so bad. It was inspiring being around nature like this, and I wished our world was closer to nature. Then again, I had noted there were more bugs inside the homes compared to my home. Was it the price to pay to be closer to nature? It made sense but made me wonder how bad the bug problem had been throughout history. It really wasn't something most people thought about. A lot of what we take for granted wasn't possible even a hundred years ago.

The sun was beginning to set behind the distant trees. I stared out at the forming sunset. Red at night, sailor's delight, so I was told. The sky was a blood red, and although it was said to be good luck, something about it felt ominous.

"We should head back. It doesn't seem like anything is here," Chase commented.

I nodded. "I suppose you are right. Hopefully we beat the others back or else they are going to give us a lot of crap."

He let out a laugh. "You can say that again. They will take it out on me more than you, however, so I wouldn't worry."

"I wouldn't be so sure. It seems like Malcolm has been cold toward me. I can't blame him though. All of this is pretty hard."

He shrugged. "Yeah, but he doesn't have to be as rude as he has been. He just needs to relax, but that executioner nature of his always gets the better of him when he's angry. He gets all cold and dark and angsty. Best to ignore him."

I nodded. "Right. I'll try."

Chase transported us to the front of the palace as ordered. I was happy he did that, as the others were gone, and I didn't want to get stabbed. Or shot.

I noticed he was a bit quieter after we left the first house. I wasn't sure if it was due to my comment about Malcolm or if it had to do with me not making my mind up about staying in Wonderland. I didn't ask as I didn't want to start another argument with him.

We were the first ones back, which made sense since Chase could teleport us across the land. I wondered how long it would take the others to get back as I was starting to get hungry. My stomach grumbled in the empty room, echoing and sounded louder than it should have. I blushed as Chase let out a laugh.

"We can go get something to eat while we wait for the others. I'm sure they wouldn't mind."

I moved a strand of my blond hair behind my ear. "Yeah, I guess that would be a good idea. Where should we go?"

Chase pondered on the thought. "How about crepes? Then we can get it to go and come back before they even return."

"That sounds like a wonderful plan to me. I love crepes."

"Well, it is Wonderland. He smirked. I rolled my eyes as he led us back outside and toward a little booth just outside the castle. I glanced over the menu. There were so many to choose from.

"I don't know what I want. I should get something savory, since it is dinner after all, but these sweet crepes sound amazing."

Chase shrugged. "Order both."

I shook my head. "No, that's too much and it will just be a waste. Besides, crepes should be eaten fresh."

"Well, we can always come back later for a dessert crepe."

"That is true. Fine. I will order the ham-and-cheese crepe!" I told the cashier.

"And I will take the tuna-salad crepe!" Chase smiled.

I gave him a disgusted look.

"What? It's yummy!"

I shook my head. "Only a cat would like that."

"Well, good thing I am a cat!"

We laughed as we waited for our crepes. Since there were a few people ahead of us, it took about fifteen minutes. Once we were handed our crepes, we headed back into the palace, taking bites of our meal as we walked.

My crepe was heavenly and reminded me that I needed to go to French Press in Salem sometime with Kate. We could study there and eat crepes. It was a win-win. It was already fall as well, so they would probably have a pumpkin-flavored one, which sounded delicious, even with a stomach that was almost full now.

We entered the meeting room to find Malcolm, Kenny, Bill, and the White Rabbit were back. Malcolm glanced at the crepes in our hands.

"I said to come straight back here."

Chase shook his head in disbelief that he was about to get scolded. "Alice was hungry, and you all weren't back yet. So I know you haven't been waiting long."

Malcolm turned away. "Whatever."

"Can I go now?" the White Rabbit asked.

Malcolm nodded. "You may."

I watched as the little boy, whom I never wanted to cross paths on a bad day, ran off toward the King and Queen's room. He never seemed to leave their side, unless he was given orders.

Kenny started jumping up and down. "Did you get me one?"

Chase shook his head. "No."

He pouted. "Aw."

I felt a little bad we didn't get them anything, but we had no idea when they would be back or what they would want. I wanted to say something, but with

Malcolm there I felt a bit awkward as things were patched up between us. So I ate in silence as we waited for Melvin and Davis to show up. About fifteen minutes passed when they walked through the door, both holding crepes. Malcolm shot them a look.

"We were hungry, and it was on the way!" Davis exclaimed. "You aren't going to make me feel guilty for eating it."

Malcolm sighed. "Whatever. Let's begin the meeting. Bill, do we need to go get the White Rabbit again?"

Bill shrugged. "Not really. He's fine where he is."

"All right. But did you two find anything?"

Bill pulled out his files. "One house was a dead end, and the other did appear to be connected to Morpheus, but it didn't have any leads to who the mastermind was. I have a feeling he was simply someone Morpheus had picked up along the way and had no contact prior to morphing into the one person we know as Morpheus." Bill laughed. "I get it now. Morph…eus."

We all chuckled. It was right in front of us. And the fact it was the name of the god of dreams. It worked two different ways.

Malcolm didn't look up from the folders he held. "Chase, what did you two find?"

Chase glanced at me, as if asking me if I wanted to talk or if he should. I gestured for him to show them the diary and to tell them about it.

"Well, two houses didn't have any clues, but one had a major clue." He pulled out the diary and note. "We found a note from the mastermind. There is no signature or anything, but we can start matching up handwriting samples to figure out who it was."

Malcolm set the folders down and stared at the diary. He seemed surprised. "You two found something…"

I nodded. "Yup. We think he was the main identity of Morpheus. Whoever is behind it used the death of his family to make him turn on Wonderland." I paused. "I can understand why. What his diary talked about was pretty tragic. It doesn't make it right, but you can feel for him, you know?"

Chase handed the note to Malcolm, and he scanned it. "This will take some time to go through. But luckily we have documents going all the way back to the Heart Kingdom."

"The diary also talks about what happened to him. I think it is important to let his community know. They have been mourning him and his family for a while and deserve answers," I commented. "The family I know told me so."

Malcolm nodded. "That can be arranged after we find out who was behind this. We don't want to alert them that we are onto something. We have no idea where they are hiding. None of this information leaves this room. Does everyone understand that? If anyone asks, we say we found nothing and have to start from scratch. This note could be from anyone in the Kingdom."

We all nodded in agreement. Chase started to grab the document when Malcolm grabbed it out of his hand.

"I will be taking this for the time being. We will need to begin going through handwriting samples. First, we will go through the most recent letters we have in our database and start ruling out everyone in the palace. Then we will look in the archives and go through those of people we haven't heard from for a while."

"There are others like you all out there?" I asked. I had thought they were the last ones with roles in Wonderland.

Bill nodded. "Yup. Quite a few retired, so to speak, and reside on the outskirts of Wonderland. There's Doris, the Dodo; Walter, the Walrus; Carl, the Cook…"

"Some have passed," Melvin added. "But a lot ran off after the fall of the Red and White Kingdom. They didn't want to go through all the problems of a Kingdom again. They all actually fought having a King and Queen, as they wanted a democracy, but were ironically out voted."

"Which gives them all motive…" I sighed.

Everyone nodded.

Malcolm answered. "I have documents they all have written though, so it won't be too bad."

"Just let me know what I need to do and I will do it,"

I said with a smile. "I am trying to become an artist, so I can help match it as well."

Malcolm checked the time. "I wouldn't want you to bore yourself when you have a lot of schoolwork coming up. I know this year is going to be a lot more difficult for you."

I wasn't sure how much time had gone by in my world. I glanced to Bill, who was the one who usually kept track of it as time changed in this world in a peculiar way.

Bill checked his watch. "It seems a few hours have gone by, Alice. You should probably head back soon, as you will need to get some sleep as well."

I nodded. "Okay. Just promise me you will come get me if something comes up."

Malcolm didn't even look at me. "I'm sure Chase will."

I glanced over at Chase, who was grinning. "Ready to head back, Alice?"

"I suppose I am." Since I was practically being forced back. I did have to deal with the problem of my parents waking up soon, but it also felt like there was something else—like Malcolm didn't want me around anymore.

Chase turned to Bill. "Do I have to go outside this time?"

"I will allow you to transfer her from her room here."

Chase held out his hand. "Come on, Alice, let's get you back to your other clothes and get some rest. We will have to get the sweet crepes another time. Then tomorrow we can meet up and go over our bio lab."

I let out a moan as I grabbed his hand. I had completely forgotten about that worksheet. It was going to take hours to complete.

Would all this work never end?

CHAPTER EIGHT

A couple of weeks went by as I waited for the others to find a match between the note and any of their old documents. There were apparently a lot of papers to go through, and Malcolm and the others were trying to not stand out while searching. They also made fake missions that they ran to keep whoever was spying on them confused. Either way, so far there was nothing.

So I focused on my studies, which was taking up all my time anyway. We weren't even close to midterms yet, and I was already feeling overwhelmed. There was so much reading, and I tried to take notes of it all, but there was so much, and it was making my head spin. All I wanted to do was take a break and paint for hours, but I barely had time outside of art class. I was glad I had at least that class to work on my craft, but as the days went, I felt the stress of it all begin to impede my creativity.

I picked at the rice in my bento as I felt like everything was weighing me down. I tried to figure out how late I would need to stay up that night as I had dance and chores to finish up, but the paper for AP European history was due later this week and I hadn't finished it yet.

"You okay, Alice?" Kate asked.

I turned to her with a thankful smile. "I'm okay. Just a little overwhelmed. I really just want to focus on art, but so far all I have had time for is homework."

Chase patted my back. "It will be okay."

Melvin and Davis were silent as they saw Chase scoot closer to me. I took a deep breath.

"Yeah, I suppose it will be once all is said and done."

He and I both knew what I meant. I still had to decide where I wanted to spend my life. Whatever I chose, I couldn't go back on it and would have to be happy with my decision.

"Do you want to hang out this weekend? We can de-stress a bit at the mall, and then you and I can get a bunch of homework done," Kate suggested. "I don't have track this weekend as it is our week off."

"That would be great, Kate. Thank you."

Chase nudged me. "It's busy season for your parents, isn't it? So we could study a bit at the coffee shop before they pick you up."

"Oh, I drove today since it's starting to get cold out and so then I could head straight home and work on my assignment. I can drive you over though, if you want. But I get to pick the music."

"Sure!" Chase grinned.

"Just make sure to head home after dance, Chase. We have a lot to get done for our project." Melvin eyed Chase.

Davis nodded in agreement. "Yeah, we won't want to kick you out of the group for not doing your share."

Chase laughed. "As if you could do anything, Davis."

Davis's cheeks turned red. "Shut up, Chase!"

I noticed in the past week they were getting more and more irritable around Chase. I wondered if it had anything to do with Wonderland. I meant to ask but hadn't found the right time yet. It was an awkward subject to bring up, not to mention Chase was always around.

"Well, I am looking forward to this weekend, Kate. And as for you three, maybe we can study a little this weekend? Like Sunday evening? We have some bio stuff coming up."

I really meant Wonderland. They all nodded in agreement.

"Yeah, we could use some help," Davis whispered.

"Sounds great."

The bell rang, and I closed up my half-eaten bento. Back to the madness we go.

I waited by my green beetle bug that was once my sister's car. Chase was taking his time at his locker. My guess was that the others were scolding him about something again. I checked my phone to find that ten minutes had already passed. If we didn't hurry, we would hit some traffic. Luckily I knew all the back roads to get around Salem traffic pretty well. That is, as long as we didn't have to go across the bridge. There was no way around that mess.

Spotting Chase with his backpack slumped over his shoulder, I unlocked the trunk for him and he threw his bag inside. He was frowning.

"You okay?" I asked as we got in the car.

He shrugged. "Whatever. Let's just get to dance."

I nodded and flipped through my playlist, starting up my favorite playlist called Pop Punk Now. It was upbeat enough to keep me going, and I hoped it would cheer up Chase, or at least get the angst out of him. "*Misery Business*" by Paramore started playing.

Chase's head started nodding with the beat.

I spun the volume dial up and started shouting the lyrics. Chase joined and we continued the chorus and started laughing as Paramore started singing the next section.

"I'm glad I got you to smile," I commented. "You looked like you were in a foul mood."

Chase shook his head. "Yeah, sorry about that. Melvin and Davis yelled at me about something."

"Oh? Something in Wonderland?"

"Forget about it. It isn't important."

I didn't push further as it was apparent he wasn't going to tell me. "So, this weekend I can come to Wonderland to help a little. It's been a while since I've been back, and I feel it might look odd if I didn't show up again for a while. We want to make them think maybe I came back to look elsewhere or something."

Chase nodded. "Yeah, I think it is a good idea. and Wonderland is more fun than this place."

"That's for sure."

"Then why not pick Wonderland? You could choose now, Alice. We could transport right now and cut the ties, and you could live the rest of your life in Wonderland."

"Well, first off, because I wouldn't want to leave a random car in the road, and second, because I don't know if I could do that to my family."

He folded his arms. "They wouldn't know. They would have forgotten that you even existed. Like Hermione's parents. They would feel no pain."

I shifted in my seat. "I don't know…"

"But if you choose Earth, then everyone in Wonderland suffers. We won't forget you, and we will have to live with the memory of you for as long as we survive, which can be centuries upon centuries."

I didn't say anything. He had a point there, but that would also mean if I picked Wonderland, I would live with the guilt of leaving this world for centuries. I was starting to see what Malcolm meant.

Regrets were worse when they were for an eternity.

We arrived at dance class, and I parked in the spot that I now considered mine. A couple of people commented on the fact that Chase and I rode together. We both rolled our eyes but didn't say anything. It would only make it worse, we found.

Dance came and went, and I messed up a few moves and almost landed on my face due to thinking about schoolwork and chores and everything. As I gathered my things and headed out the door, Chase ran up.

"Wait, Alice!"

"Hey, what is it?"

He grinned. "I was wondering if I could come over and we could study for a bit—at least until your parents come home."

I glanced around to make sure no one heard him. Luckily no one was within hearing distance. In Wonderland it was normal for us to hang out without supervision, but in this world, it had different connotations.

"Umm… I have a lot of work."

"I will help, I swear!" He gave me the most Puss in Boots-like stare he could.

"Fine, let's head home."

He went over and grabbed his stuff. With a smile, he joined me in my car.

"Weren't you supposed to head straight back to Wonderland to help with going through the letters?"

"Meh, they can do that without me."

"Well, don't say I didn't warn you."

I resumed the playlist we were listening to earlier. The song "*Rabbit Hole*" by Blink-182 started playing. I laughed.

"So applicable," Chase commented.

"It's a punk playlist. Wonderland is a place of dreams for everyone. It's an escape that no one thinks is real."

"I wonder what would happen if they knew everything."

"I don't think anyone would believe, or not many anyway. Some would of course, but not one's people would listen to."

We traveled across Salem, which took a good thirty minutes at this time of the day. I was able to take back roads most of the way, which helped. I parked the car and unlocked the front door.

"Want anything to eat? I think we have some leftovers that I was supposed to heat up for dinner."

"Sure, if there is enough."

I nodded. "There is. I will just need to heat it up. Make yourself at home meanwhile. My parents won't be home for an hour or so."

"Anything I can help with?"

I bit my lip. "If you don't mind doing the dishes and taking out the trash, that would be perfect. Then I won't have to worry about it later."

He smiled. "Consider it done!"

Chase started doing the dishes while I gathered up the food. Once I reheated it in the microwave, he already had the sink emptied and everything was in the dishwasher.

"I will gather the trash after we eat."

"Thank you so much, Chase! Here's the food."

"Ooh, leftover Chinese food. That's always the best."

I shrugged. "I mean, Chinese food is always better the first time around. Crunchier and less soggy."

"Well, I don't mind it."

We ate the leftovers and glanced over the readings that were due tomorrow. I let out a sigh.

Chase squeezed my hand. "We will get through it all, don't worry."

I grabbed my head as if I were about to pull out my hair. "Easy for you to say—in the end, you don't have to worry about your grades. My parents want straight As. It's just not fair. I'm not a smart student."

"You are very smart! Just not school smart, but that isn't everything. Your society is very confusing on that, by the way. They think school is the only way to learn, and even then that doesn't cover many topics. You have defeated a villain and saved a whole world. You are practically a sailor scout."

I laughed a little. It made sense, but how would I tell my parents that? It's not like they would understand. Chase grabbed my hand.

"Seriously, you have a lot of great qualities. Just because there are some things you don't understand doesn't mean you aren't smart. You will figure it out eventually."

"Thanks." I bit my lip and closed the book. "But you are right—cramming isn't going to do anything. I'm going to paint a little to help get my mind off things."

Chase nodded. "Yeah! I haven't watched you paint in forever."

"I didn't think it was much to watch."

He shrugged. "I think it's fun."

We moved to my bedroom, and I pulled out some

watercolor paper and my palette. I went to fill a cup with water and brought it back.

"What are you going to paint?" Chase asked as he sat on my bed.

I shrugged. "I don't know, probably an animal… I think a fox."

I knew I would just do something simple, and nothing with my detail as I didn't have too much time. I mainly just wanted to get my frustrations out and calm myself. About half an hour passed, and I was finished. It turned out better than I expected, and I knew I would have to bring it to school to have my art teacher critique it.

"Wow, Alice! You always amaze me."

I blushed, almost forgetting that Chase was there. "Thanks. You didn't have to stay all this time, especially if the others are waiting for you."

He shrugged. "I don't really want to meet up with them anytime soon. Long story."

I took a seat next to him. "Oh… Well, my parents will be home soon, so you will have to head back to Wonderland…"

"You could come with." Chase's eyes turned bright.

"I thought I was coming this weekend."

"I mean forever… You looked so happy not working on schoolwork—you could do that forever in Wonderland."

"Chase, I—"

Before I could finish, Chase leaned in and kissed me. I was surprised and quickly moved back.

"What are you—?"

"Alice!" my mother's voice called. "Are you in your room?"

Chase disappeared before either of us could discuss what happened. I let out a breath as I stared where he once was.

"Crap."

CHAPTER NINE

Chase and I didn't talk about what happened last night but faked everything being fine and normal. I was too afraid to bring it up again, and I felt my reaction must have answered his question of whether or not I had feelings for him. It wasn't that I didn't like him—he was a great friend—but I just didn't feel that way about him. I still had feelings for Malcolm, and my heart felt that if I moved on to Chase, I would be causing even more problems.

Especially if I did pick Wonderland.

How awkward would it be if I were in a relationship with Chase for centuries in front of Malcolm? They were already on bad terms with each other, and I had a feeling this would send Malcolm over the edge. Then again, if Malcolm really cared, why didn't he ask me to stay with him in Wonderland?

I had to keep reminding myself Malcolm didn't want me there because of what a long life like that does to the mind. He's lived for centuries now. I wasn't able to comprehend what that would be like, and if I considered it a mistake, I would never be able to live with myself and yet would have centuries to feel miserable.

The drama did not help my stress about school. I could barely concentrate during class as I kept thinking about whether or not that was why Melvin and Davis were mad at him and why they were giving him crap. Did they know about his feelings for me? Malcolm always seemed to glare when the two of us were together. Was I just blind to Chase's feelings for me all this time?

Friday was now here, and I could spend the rest of the weekend with Kate. I debated on telling her what happened, but I needed a sounding board—I needed to know whether I was an idiot all along. She would be frank too, which would hurt, but I needed it right then.

Mr. Lewis handed out the end-of-the-week quiz, and

I stared at it like it was in some kind of foreign language. This was an open-note quiz—I couldn't fail it, right? I gaped at the words, confused as to what it was trying to say.

Why did this look like a blank page with nothing on it? Why did it seem all white but also with words that made no sense? Was this Norse? Were these runes? Kanji? Sanskrit? They all just looked like lines with no meaning. I tried to slow down my breathing and focus.

Kate kicked me under the table, as she must have noticed my momentary panic attack. This snapped me out of whatever trance I was in, and I was able to focus. The lines became words, and I let out the breath I had been holding. I scanned my notes, wishing that my handwriting was a little better, but was able to fill out all the questions before the bell rang.

"All right, class, turn in your quizzes and have a great weekend! My hope is to grade all your essays by the end of next week, so check Canvas for your grades and critiques."

I had stayed up late the night before, working on the paper, and tried to make sure all my sources were cited and that my points made sense. Kate said I was worrying too much about the paper and needed to only give it two good look-overs, instead of the half dozen I had last night, but I couldn't help it since it was a good chunk of our grade. I ended up writing on how the art of the Renaissance was the leading force of bringing Europe out of the Middle Ages. Mr. Lewis was the one who suggested it, and it seemed interesting enough. I figured since it would be about art, that I would have more passion in my writing, but sometimes I got carried away and my points would start to blur together.

As we stepped out into the hallway, Kate pulled me aside. Other students passed us, trying to get to class before the next bell rang.

"Hey, are you doing okay? You have seemed to be out of it these past few days."

I gave her my most innocent smile. "Yeah, I'm fine. I've just had a lot going on with everything… We can discuss it this weekend."

She furrowed her eyebrows. "Okay, but know I'm here if you need me."

"Thank you, but I will be fine. I can wait until tomorrow. And I don't really want anyone overhearing."

"That bad, huh?"

I laughed. "Maybe a little. I better get to my next class. See ya!" I headed to my locker and changed out my books, taking deep breaths and wishing this day would just end so I could hang out with Kate this weekend. Time didn't move fast in this world, no matter how much I wanted it to. Closing my locker, I headed toward my next class.

* * *

The rest of the morning went as smoothly as it could. By the time lunch came, I was tired and ready to go home and sleep until Saturday. I had dance, however, and just hoped I wouldn't accidentally fall or something from my drowsiness. I debated skipping but didn't want to get in trouble with Becca. We had a performance in a couple of months, and I needed to perfect my solo part.

I sighed as I set my bento down and realized I was craving something sweet. Today there was some cobbler available at the cafeteria, so I got in line to buy some. I deserved a snack after the week I had, and since I rarely used my allowance these days, I knew I could splurge for the two-dollar dessert.

Coming back to the table, I found that Chase, Melvin, and Davis had all taken their seats. I took my normal seat next to Chase but didn't really glance over to him. I didn't know how to act around him any longer. Was I getting too close to him and that was why he thought I had feelings for him? Or did he just hope for the best? We still hadn't discussed it, and yet he seemed as normal as could be, which made me even more frustrated. How could he pretend like everything was fine? I wished I could be as carefree as him.

"So, decided on getting something sweet today?" Chase asked as he saw the slight cold shoulder I had given him. He tried to act like he didn't care, but I could tell in his eyes that he was taken aback by it. I shouldn't have been such a jerk, but I was also still really mad at him. I glanced over to Melvin and Davis, who were watching us closely.

I took a deep breath and tried to regain any normality I could muster. "Yeah, just been a long week and need to get through the rest of the day and dance."

"We could always go to the coffee shop before class and get some caffeine."

"Perhaps. Although Becca doesn't like me being hyper during class… not since last time we went and got coffee and I almost broke my leg on the balance beam."

Chase laughed. "I forgot about that! Good thing I was there to catch you, huh?"

I nodded slowly. "Yeah, I guess so."

Melvin watched me suspiciously as I knew I probably looked uneasy and had been blowing Chase off all day, and this was not helping. I tried to act normal, but between the stress of school, my stomach hurting, and being hungry at the same time, I was doing my best to keep from not curling up in a ball and crying.

The rest of lunch was rather quiet, and I ate my meal in peace. Although the cobbler hit the spot, I decided it was one of the worst cobblers I had ever had and knew I wouldn't be spending my allowance to buy it again. I cleaned my plate off before setting it in the dirty dish container as Chase ran off to go get the books he forgot for next class. As I turned around, I found Melvin and Davis standing behind me.

I jumped and glanced between the two of them. They just stared. "Uh, hi?"

Melvin hesitated. "Did something happen with you and Chase?"

Crap. I shook my head. "No. Nothing, why?"

"You seem off," Davis remarked. "Like you feel awkward."

I shrugged. "I don't know what you two are talking about."

"Sure…" Melvin sighed. "Which tells me he did."

"Nothing happened. And besides, would it matter? It's not like Malcolm is going to come back. He made it clear he doesn't want me to stay in Wonderland."

I regretted saying that, but it was the truth. I didn't see why they cared when Malcolm had been pushing me away, other than the fact that Chase wanted me to stay in Wonderland. They seemed to side with Malcolm and wanted me to stay on Earth.

"Alice…," Davis began, but I shook my head.

"Forget about it. I get it. I know there is more to this than just my stupid feelings, okay? I will come help you guys this weekend, and then you all won't have to deal with my teen drama any longer."

I turned and headed to my next class. Neither of them stopped me but let me run off like a stupid teenaged girl.

Ugh, why did all this have to get more complicated?

This was so awkward.

Not only did I have to go to dance with Chase, whom I would be touching since we had an act together, everyone was still commenting on how close we were and the fact that I brought him over in my car. I didn't want to just leave him at school and make him transport when we had already established a sort of car-riding ritual now. I stayed quiet the entire ride over, and Chase didn't say anything but sang to the music I had been playing. I tried to sing along as well but was having trouble juggling the music, the circle of stress in my mind, and making sure I didn't run a red light.

The worst part was having to dance with him since were very close in those moments. It didn't used to be awkward, as we had practiced these moves a million times, but now that he kissed me, wanting to bring our relationship to a level I wasn't comfortable with, being this close was strange. I prayed that Becca didn't notice and that the other students wouldn't ask if something had happened. I would probably turn red and not be able to answer in a convincing matter.

After class, I headed to my car and tried to get out of

there before Chase stopped me or tried to tag along. Although he could easily transport into my room, he hadn't since the kiss, so I knew he understood I needed some space.

Except I watched as he came running over as I unlocked my car. I let out a sigh.

"Alice! Hey, do you want to go to the mall and kill some time? I mean, it's Friday and you shouldn't work too hard. There's something to be said for those who work and don't play."

I shook my head. "Nah, I better not. I want to get some painting done before this weekend. Kate and I are doing homework tomorrow, and then we will be going to Wonderland later, right?"

He nodded, his eyes a bit sad. "Yeah, we will. I guess that makes sense you need to practice what you want to have a career in. I will see you later."

With that, he turned toward the warehouses to transport back to Wonderland. I took a deep breath and let it out slowly. This was going to be a long weekend.

CHAPTER TEN

"Ugh!" I yelled into the pillow I brought over to Kate's house.

She watched as I rolled around her bed, letting out my frustrations of the week. "Wow, I haven't seen you get this frustrated since they threw you that curveball in that one manga you read."

"You mean *Black Butler*? I still can't believe that happened. Great, now I'm thinking about that too. And here I thought my brain couldn't take any more frustrations." I kicked my feet against the bed. "Ugh!"

"Tell me what's wrong."

I let out a sigh as I rolled over and sat up. "Besides

school being hard, wanting to stay in dance class, and having no time to paint?"

She folded her arms. "While I know you are frustrated with all those things this year, I feel like there is something else bothering you. Are you going to tell me, or am I going to have to get it out of you?"

I grabbed my pillow and moaned into it. "Ugh!"

"That bad, huh?"

"I just… I don't even know where to start. I mean… I just… Ugh!"

She sighed. "Just tell me what happened between you and Chase."

I frowned and turned my head to face her. "How did you know it was about Chase?"

Kate rolled her eyes. "Because you have been giving him the cold shoulder all week. I'm not blind."

I collapsed back down on her bed. "Chase kissed me."

"About time," she commented and then coughed. "Sorry, I mean… Well?"

"Well? Did you know he liked me?" I exclaimed.

Kate held back a laugh. "Everyone but you knew he liked you. It's obvious, Alice. He was flirting with you even when you were with Malcolm."

"He was?" I asked as I leaned back up. "That would explain some of the tension between them two."

"Yeah, just a bit. I'm surprised the two of them never

got into a real brawl."

Oh, they had. Now it made more sense. But there was also the fact that they didn't like each other before I came along. "I just don't know what to do…" I sighed. "There's so much going on right now that I just…"

"Well, what about it scares you? I mean, to me, other than the fact he's a troublemaker, it seems like you like Chase, and the two of you get along and are with each other constantly. Why don't you want to move it a step further?"

Because Wonderland makes everything a bit more complicated. "I don't know… I mean, he is a cool guy and I like him a lot, but I just never thought of him that way, you know?"

"What if you did?"

I let out a breath. "It just feels wrong, like I'm betraying—" I stopped, realizing what I was about to say. The real reason I didn't want to return Chase's feelings was because I still loved Malcolm.

"You feel like you are betraying Malcolm? So? Screw that guy! He left practically overnight to Colorado. Why would you feel like you were betraying him if he is completely out of your life?"

There was the problem—Malcolm wasn't out of my life, but I couldn't explain that. I didn't want to seem like I was just hanging on to him even though he was gone because he really wasn't. All if it was so complicated. I bit my lip.

"He's out of your life, right? You haven't been texting him, have you?"

I shook my head. "No, I haven't. I guess it's got more to do with after high school. Chase wants to move far away, and I don't know if I would be up for that."

She raised an eyebrow. "Far away? I thought you wanted out of Oregon. Wouldn't that be your wish?"

I shrugged, trying to come up with a good comparison. "I mean yeah, but like, he wants to move really far, like England or something."

"Would you not want to move to England?"

"It would be cool, but could I do that to my family? What if I didn't have enough money to visit often and didn't see them much? And you— What if I moved far away and we didn't see each other?"

Kate smiled. "Alice, this is why you have a heart of gold. You worry too much about other people and don't think about what you want. Do you want to move far away? Would it make you happy?"

"I-I don't know. I feel so overwhelmed about what to do next that I feel like I'm almost stuck. Do you ever get that feeling?"

She nodded. "Of course. We all do. We are still in high school. Heck, my mother says she gets it still."

My parents would never admit something like that to me. They wouldn't understand my worries like Kate's mom. "I love your family—they are so caring and understanding."

"Yeah, I bet it doesn't help when your parents aren't very open and care about school more than, well, anything."

I let out a sigh. "Yeah, that isn't helping either."

"Well, I am sure my parents will adopt you if you needed it."

I laughed. "Thanks. That makes me feel a little better."

"And you could always run away to England. That will show them."

"Yeah… I guess I could."

We sat there in silence for a while. I began to think—what would Wonderland be like? If I lived there for the rest of time, would I be happy? I would have my friends—all except Kate. Everyone in this world would forget I would have ever existed, so it wasn't like I would be hurting them, right? Maybe I did need to give it more thought.

Kate snapped her fingers. "Hey, how about we go to French Press and get some crepes? And study there for a bit."

I jumped up. "Yes! I was going to suggest crepes, but I totally spaced. It has been a long week."

"Well, good thing I suggested it. And I think they have pumpkin crepes right now, which I know is your favorite."

I grinned. "Yes, they are! I will drive! And then we can go to Escape Fiction since it's just down the street."

She grabbed her pink coat that had been thrown on the end of her bed. "Of course. What's crepes without books?"

We got into my beetle bug and headed toward Commercial Street. On the weekend, the streets weren't too busy, but there were quite a few people hanging out at the creperie, enjoying their Saturday afternoon. Kate and I were able to find a table, however, and went up to order. I ordered the pumpkin spice crepe, and she got the strawberry custard. I also got a hot black chai to keep me awake while we tackled through the readings and busy work for the week.

The crepes at the French Press were huge. Like, way larger than the ones in Wonderland. The crepe I had last week was manageable and easy to carry, whereas the ones here covered an entire plate and then some. Luckily, working on homework so much gave me an appetite, and I would more than likely finish it. It always amazed Kate, as she generally took half of hers to go. I also didn't believe crepes tasted good being heated up again, so I forced myself to finish it. It probably wasn't the healthiest thing for me, but since I didn't eat here too often, I didn't worry about it. Besides, with how much training I did between dance and fighting in Wonderland, I was definitely burning those calories and staying fit.

I opened up my European history textbook and started reading the chapter on the Romans invading Britain. I found the leader Boudica to be quite amazing and powerful. With all the conquests Caesar did, or tried to do, it was no wonder he was murdered. It seemed that he didn't care at what cost his conquests had.

After we finished the first chapter, I went and ordered another tea. Kate and I discussed the outline and questions Mr. Lewis had given us to make sure we read the chapter. Most of them were easy, but there was always one that threw me for a loop. Kate easily explained it to me.

"Man, Kate, I wish I could come to conclusions like you do. I feel I overthink everything." I sighed.

"I wouldn't be able to come up with the images you draw and paint, so believe me when I say we each have our own talents."

I laughed. "That's fair. I do love to draw."

"That you do. And you will get the hang of this year's workload, don't worry. We will come here often to study, as crepes seem to be your brain food."

"That they are!"

The café quieted down, and I debated getting a savory crepe for dinner but remembered that Kate's mom was going to make shepherd's pie for dinner. Her dinners were always the best, and although I did love crepes, I preferred her cooking to any restaurant in Salem.

Since we also wanted to go to Escape Fiction, we finished up on the chapter we were in the middle of and packed up to head over before dinner. Mrs. B. always had dinner ready at seven, so we still had two hours to kill at the bookstore or a little less since we needed to drive back. I unlocked my beetle bug, and we climbed in. Kate glanced over to me.

"Would you move to England?" she commented. "To be with Chase?"

I blinked, startled. "Um, I don't know. I don't know if I feel about him that way… But maybe?" It wouldn't be England—I meant Wonderland when I said that. "I mean, moving-wise. Going far away sounds nice. Why?"

She shrugged. "It's just strange to think of you in an entirely different country. It would be cool though."

"Yeah, it would be cool. Whatever I pick, though, it will be away from this place. I don't feel I fit in."

"I understand that. You need somewhere you can connect to and have a home, so to speak. Honestly, I couldn't see you settling down anywhere."

"Oh? What do you mean?"

"I mean, you are so artistic and love learning about

everything. Your parents act like school is the only place to learn, but you are so good at learning people's stories and seeing everything as an adventure. You need somewhere where you can be like that—a place that will never bore you."

Although I liked her comment, it made me feel a bit sad. I did have a place like that—it was Wonderland. But was choosing Wonderland that easy? It wasn't like I could communicate that with anyone in this world, nor could I really explain my problem. And I wouldn't be able to explore this world if I chose Wonderland. However, that took money, whereas in Wonderland it seemed like I could go to anywhere I wanted without having to worry about such things. Especially with Chase since he could transport anywhere, although I did like the adventure of traveling on foot, except in the Dark Forest.

I guess I would figure it out eventually. I just would hate to pick the wrong choice and have to live the rest of my life with regret.

Starting up my car, we headed over toward Escape Fiction. I pushed all thoughts of Wonderland behind me, and those of school, and focused on finding a new good read. Then I would get so engrossed in the book that I would put off doing homework and cause even more problems.

Yeah, that sounded like a plan.

CHAPTER ELEVEN

The sleepover with Kate lifted my spirits, and I felt
ready for anything. I still didn't know what my choice
would be, but with Kate explaining to me how I needed
to do what I thought was right for me, I felt more
confident.

It was Sunday evening, which was the only day I had
a sit-down meal with my parents. Although I didn't feel
connected to them, I did appreciate moments like those
as many families didn't get to have dinners together.
Tonight we were having pesto pasta with roasted

chicken and vegetables. I made the pesto sauce and had fun stuffing all the basil leaves from our little plant into the food processor. Add some oil, garlic, pine nuts, lemon juice, and presto—pesto.

Once dinner was ready, we sat at the table. It was quiet now that Lilith and Edith were off to college. I liked it, as then I wouldn't get into arguments with them, but it also meant that all the attention was on me at the dinner table. I wasn't sure which was worse. More than likely, fighting with my sisters as I usually ran to my room angry.

"How are your classes coming along?" my father asked as he took a sip of his white wine. It had a fancy name, but I never remembered it. There were so many wines across the Willamette Valley that it was kind of ridiculous. Beautiful, but ridiculous.

I shrugged. "They are going. They all have a lot of busy work, and it's hard to juggle it all."

"Well, maybe you should cut dance after school then."

I clenched my fork. Here we go again. "No, I can manage dance fine. I need it to make sure I stay active and have a mental rest. It all should end up okay."

"I'm sure you will do fine, darling." My mother cut her piece of chicken. "But do remember, school comes first."

Actually, Wonderland came first in my mind. I took

another bite of my pasta. "I took in one of my paintings to my art teacher. She said I did a really nice job using watercolors and thinks I have what it takes to become a professional artist."

"A professional artist?" Father laughed. "Is that a thing now?"

I let out a sigh. I wanted to tell them about my achievements—just like my sisters did at the table—but nothing I did ever compared to them. Nothing I did ever mattered. But I went on to tell them anyway. "It is. She said she would help me make my portfolio for trying to get scholarships. She also gave me a list of colleges I could apply to."

"That's nice, dear," my mother commented. She didn't seem to be listening, and my father had grown bored with the conversation as well and sipped at his wine some more. Neither of them considered art to be a real degree. I didn't know why I kept on trying to talk to them about it.

"How is your friend Kate doing? She seems like a smart girl," my mother asked. At least they liked Kate, since Kate was actually quite smart and helped me on a lot of things.

"She is doing good. We got a lot of work done. They might be going to State this year, which will be great. I might want to tag along and root her on, but I'm not sure where it is going to be held this year. I was going to carpool with her mom."

"Is she able to juggle all that with school?"

I nodded. "Yup. She's doing good at school. We are excited for European history. It's only about a month until we go over to Europe."

"That's right, you won't be home for Thanksgiving when your sisters are home," father commented. "They are going to miss you."

No, they aren't. "I guess… I just hope it snows somewhere we go. That would be cool. It has been a while since it has snowed here."

"Don't speak too soon, dear. The winter hasn't even started, and they believe this is going to be a cold one."

I did not want to experience driving in the snow. Normally school was closed if it snowed, so I doubted I would have any trouble, but it still scared me. At least my parents would probably just drop me off those days.

We all finished dinner, and I had to do the dishes since it was my night to do them. I cleaned them all off and stuck them in the dishwasher as my parents sat on the couch to watch their latest show—*The Good Place* —which was a funny show, but I was going to wait for it all to be on Netflix and binge it with Kate some time.

After taking out the trash, I retired to my room for the night and finished up the biology readings, as Kate didn't have biology class. Later, in Wonderland, Chase and I would work on our lab report, or at least I hoped we would since it was due tomorrow, which wasn't really tomorrow depending on how many days we stayed in Wonderland. I had a couple of hours before Chase would come get me and we'd teleport there.

My heart started to race at the thought of Chase. Did I like him? Or was I just afraid of our awkward relationship now? I didn't hate him, and the thought of him in my life was a pleasant one, but I didn't feel the same for him like I had with Malcolm. Like I still did with Malcolm. Was it because he and Malcolm were completely different people and so I wouldn't feel the same thing even if it was love? When I thought of Malcolm, there was a comforting feeling, as if he would always hold me close and keep me safe. But when I thought of Chase, I thought of all the fun and adventures we had. He always brought a smile to my face, but could I see myself with him?

He enjoyed a lot of the same things I did and had always been there for me. Heck, he joined dance class with me. Everyone apparently knew he liked me, even the people at dance. Had I been stupid this entire time?

I shook my head. This really wasn't the time to think about it—not when Wonderland was still in danger, and I didn't know if he would even be a part of my life in a few months.

After finishing up my biology readings, I decided to paint a little before I needed to pack up for Wonderland.

I wanted to paint a watercolor again, as my teacher said I should work on them some more. After debating on what to paint, I went with one of my anime crushes, Sesshōmaru. He was just so adorable I couldn't help but love him. I felt his arc in *Inuyasha* was the most developed, and I thought he was rather cute as a teen in the third movie, so I went with that style and kimono—the one with pink flowers.

Thankfully, working on this painting and smiling nonstop as I looked up pictures of Sesshōmaru for reference made me forget my problems for a little while and my mind was able to rest. That was one thing I loved about art and anime—it helped me relaxed if even for an instant. Many people didn't understand the importance of that, and I wished I could show them. Perhaps that was why I loved art.

Once I was finished, I set aside the painting to dry and glanced around my messy room. Sighing, I quickly organized my art station and then threw all my dirty clothes in the hamper. I was bummed to find that I hadn't washed my favorite dress and would have to bring something else to Wonderland.

I quietly packed a bag of some essentials—my biology homework and lab book especially—and then some clothes in case we had some free time. I also brought a couple of manga to read, the newest *Oresama Teacher*. I couldn't believe there were only going to be a few more books until it was over. I couldn't wait to read what happened.

As I finished packing my bag, there was a knock on the door. "Alice, are you getting ready for bed?" my mother asked through the door.

"Yes, Mom," I lied. "Going to bed early and getting a good night's rest before school tomorrow."

"Good night then, sweetheart."

"Good night!" I called out.

I checked my Tardis clock. It was almost ten, and Chase would be here any minute. I grabbed my bag of snacks and water bottle and waited.

Taking a deep breath, I hoped traveling to Wonderland this time wouldn't be awkward and that we would find whoever was behind this. The only problem was once we found out who it was, would they need me anymore? Would I be kicked out of Wonderland?

I knew that it wasn't because they wanted me gone—Davis and Melvin made that clear—but that they didn't want to interfere with my life choices. But they had become such a great part of my life, I couldn't imagine going on without them. My heart began to ache at the thought. I also couldn't imagine life without my family and Kate. I couldn't choose who I cared about more, as it was different types of love. What was I going to do?

As I heard my parents' door close for the night and I tucked my anime pillow in for the night, I sensed someone appear behind me. I turned to find Chase standing there with a grin on his face.

"Ready, Alice?" he whispered.

I nodded. "Yeah, I am."

He raised an eyebrow. "Is something wrong?"

Duh, but I wasn't going to say it. "Just don't know if this is my last time to Wonderland, you know? If we find out who is behind everything, then I don't have a reason to go back. I mean, my seventeenth birthday is in a few months, and then I won't be able to go to Wonderland ever again."

He frowned a little. "I don't... I..." He stopped. "You have to make a choice, but let's not think about it right now. Even if we find who is behind this, you are still welcome to come to Wonderland. Don't worry. I will make sure of it... Until..."

I smiled. "Thanks. That means a lot." I glanced around the room to make sure everything was set and then turned off my lamp. "Let's go to Wonderland."

CHAPTER TWELVE

Traveling to Wonderland was a nice change of pace for me for the week. I could be myself—I wasn't living a lie and could speak freely. Granted, I didn't speak freely to Chase about the kiss, but that was more because it was awkward than I felt I would be judged. We appeared in the random closet-storage room in the Garden District, per normal. When we stepped outside, we found that it was nighttime, which I was thankful for as I wanted to sleep. I didn't like pulling all-nighters, even if they were in Wonderland.

"Now to the palace!" Chase said as he grabbed my arm.

"In front of it, not in it," I commented.

He rolled his catlike eyes. "Fine. Whatever."

We appeared in front of the palace. I glanced around and found that there were still quite a few people in the street, which meant that it was early night, most likely around the same time as it had been in my world. I was thankful for that as then I wouldn't have to try to mentally align with the time again.

"Should we find the others before heading to our rooms? They might still be up working," I said.

Chase nodded, his purple catlike ears twitching. "Yeah, I suppose we should. They are probably still in the library since, well, that is where all the old documents are."

My eyes widened. I absolutely loved the library. It was larger than any I had ever seen. The room felt like a pocket of space, like the Tardis, and didn't quite make sense for how big it was compared to the rest of palace and looking at it from the outside. I could live in there, absorbing all the information they had gathered through the centuries. It reminded me a lot of the library in *Avatar: The Last Airbender*, but luckily there was no grumpy owl.

We stepped into the library, and my heart felt happy for once during this long week, besides when I painted

Sesshōmaru. Books lined the shelves, perfectly waiting for someone to read them. My goal was to read as many as I could, but I knew that wouldn't be possible in the next few months. Did I have this library as one of my pros of staying in Wonderland? Perhaps.

I spotted Malcolm on the other side of the library. We both stared at each other for a moment, and then he looked away. The happy feeling in my heart quickly vanished as Chase and I ventured to him. Melvin and Davis were with him, and they had an enormous amount of papers scattered on the table.

"How does the search go?" I asked as I sat down. Chase took a seat next to me.

Malcolm gestured to the table. "This pretty much sums it all up. There are a lot of notes to go through, not to mention progress is slow since we want to make it look like we are still searching for a lead. Bill and Kenny are on a fake mission to the Heart Kingdom for something right now and are supposed to make it appear real, but my guess is they are just fooling around somewhere out there."

That was definitely true. "Well, what do you want me to do?"

He shrugged. "I'm not sure yet. I was thinking tomorrow you could travel through parts of the Kingdom, look through more houses, maybe interview people. It would be sort of a fake mission, but you never know what might pop up."

I glanced over the papers. "I can always help with going through handwriting comparison. I do have a knack for examining art and all that."

"Yes, but then those who are responsible might wonder why you are just staying in the library and might be suspicious. It's best for you to confuse and deter them for now. Once we get closer, then you can help finalize everything." Malcolm pinched the bridge of his nose. "And besides, looking at all these papers can start to eat away your brain."

I stood up. "Then let's go get some food. I could always go for dessert, and I'm sure that you all haven't eaten yet even though it is late."

Davis looked over to Malcolm with large eyes. "Please? Can we go eat now? I'm starving…"

Melvin added. "It would be nice to eat out all together."

Malcolm seemed hesitant. We generally didn't go out to eat together since we'd broken up. It was rather awkward as I felt the others wished he was there. It wasn't my fault he was being childish about it, but I never said anything. He could make his own choices, as he tried his hardest to minimize any time we had together. "Fine. We can all go out together."

I smiled, a little glad to have some time together. I glanced to Chase to find him not exactly smiling but not frowning either. He seemed more worried than anything. I ignored it, as I had a feeling it had to do with what happened earlier this week. He was also childish for ignoring it, but I supposed I should have brought it up by now. But the more time that passed, the harder it was.

The three of them gathered their papers in a pile and put them somewhere they could come back to but away from any prying eyes. Chase and I waited as we didn't want to accidentally mess up their order. We had no idea what piles meant what, and it would take more time for them to explain to us than if they just did it themselves. Once they were done, we headed out the door.

"What do you want to eat, Alice?" Davis asked.

I shrugged. "I already had dinner, so I am game for wherever you all want to go. Then I will just get something light or sweet. Or both."

"Taco shop it is!" Melvin raised a fist in the air. I laughed, as he seemed to like tacos. If he got to pick the food, he always wanted tacos. I couldn't complain, as who didn't love tacos? And they had some of the best churros I ever had, even better than the ones I had at Disneyland when I was little.

We entered the taco shop wand found it to be not too busy this late at night. We got a seat in back, and I sat next to Chase, and Malcolm sat in the spot farthest away from me. I ordered some churros, and the rest ordered some form of taco. We were all quiet as we waited for the food.

This was so awkward. I fidgeted with my jacket sleeves and looked down at the table. I didn't know why I thought it would be like old times when both Malcolm and I were clearly hurting. We wanted to be friends, but there was still the feeling deep in our hearts, or at least that was how I saw it. If he didn't feel for me any longer, then he would be fine with me around, right? He wouldn't be so quiet and trying to ignore me.

Then there was Chase. He seemed more frustrated than anything else, and Melvin and Davis just didn't want to get in the middle of any of it, so they stayed quiet.

"So…" Malcolm finally spoke. "How are this year's classes for everyone?"

I looked up. He really seemed to be trying, which made me feel better. I glanced around, but it looked as if the others wanted me to speak.

"Really stressful." I sighed. "AP classes are going to be the death of me. I barely have time to paint at home, and I'm afraid I'm not going to be able to juggle grades and dance. I'm trying really hard though."

"You will pull through. You always do."

I nodded, but it definitely didn't feel that way. I felt more like everything was going to collapse and I was going to mess up everything I worked hard for. And the thing I worked hardest for was Wonderland, which would disappear from my life completely.

Dinner arrived, and we ate our meals. The churros, yet again, were to die for. I wished I could learn how to make them every day. Everyone else seemed to enjoy their tacos, which wasn't a surprise because who didn't enjoy a taco. It was pretty rare to have a bad one. Even Jack in the Box's grease-dripping tacos were satisfying, but I figured that was because they put something addicting in them. They never did look like their photos though, let's be real.

We were mostly quiet as we ate. Us all sitting together reminded me of school last year, but those days were over. At least Malcolm agreed to come out, and we got to spend a little time together. I mainly focused on my food though, and so did the others. Once we were done, we headed back to the palace.

"Alice, we are going to look through some more files, but feel free to get some sleep. Tomorrow will be another long day, and I don't want you to put too much stress on yourself," Malcolm said gently.

I smiled. I knew he still cared even if he wasn't trying to. "Thanks. I will take you up on that offer. I will see you all in the morning?"

Everyone nodded.

"Good night!" I said as I turned toward my room and

headed down the hallway with my bag. I entered my room and turned on the light, finding the stuff I left in this world still in its place. I sighed as I threw my bag on the couch and changed out of my clothes. As I grabbed my nightshirt, I heard a knock on the door.

"Who is it?" I called as I pulled the bobby pins out of my hair.

"It's me." I heard Chase's voice answer.

I debated on answering but ended up opening the door to find him appearing nervous. His hair was a mess, and he didn't quite look me in the eyes.

"What is it?"

"Can I come in? I don't want anyone overhearing."

I nodded and he stepped in. I closed the door.

"Alice… I…" He looked away. "I wanted to tell you I care about you and that I think we should run away."

I laughed, as if he had said some kind of joke. "You can't be serious. What about the others?"

He shook his head. "Screw them. They don't appreciate you like I do. They think you should stay in your world, but I care about you enough to know you should stay here. Every time it comes up, they shut it down. But if we just hid—if we cut ties to your world, we could live life how we want in Wonderland."

I couldn't believe what I was hearing. He was being serious. Did he really think that would work? Did he think we could just disappear?

"Chase, I don't want to live my life on the run."

He grabbed my hands. "Then what are you going to do? What if they don't let you stay? What if you are forced to choose your world?"

"I-I don't know. I'm still not sure which world I would choose. I mean, I love it here—"

"Then stay!" he pleaded.

We were both silent. I truly did want to stay, as I felt I belonged here. But that didn't mean I was going to run away with Chase.

"I will make my decision, but I'm not going to hide from the others to do it."

"It's all because of Malcolm, isn't it?" He shook his head. "How can you still care for him after the two of you broke up?"

"Because I just… I don't know, okay? He was always there for me, and I think he feels the same about me still. It's just all so complicated."

"Alice, I have always been there as well! Why can't it be me?"

"Chase, I—"

He moved forward and kissed me. I froze, not expecting him to do this again. Once my mind snapped out of it, I pushed him back.

"Chase!"

He shoved past me and left me in my room, slamming the door closed behind himself. I felt tears start to form in my eyes. Why did everything become so complicated? Why couldn't we just go back to when we first defeated Morpheus?

Sighing, I collapsed on my bed and curled up in a ball. This wasn't fair. And all I wanted was Malcolm here, comforting me.

CHAPTER THIRTEEN

I woke up in a haze. It felt like I hadn't even slept but as if I had closed my eyes and opened them again and it was already morning. The only reason I knew I had indeed slept for a while was the fact my face was dry from the tears I had shed until I fell into a slumber.

Chase had tried to kiss me again.

Why was he so adamant about running away? Why didn't he want to stay with the others? I mean, I knew that the four of them had their differences, but to run away from it all… Was that even possible? Wouldn't someone eventually find us in Wonderland? I knew Malcolm would, as he was one of the best trackers in all the Kingdoms, or so he said. I had a feeling, after seeing him in the Dark Forest, that he wasn't joking about that.

While I knew Chase didn't like doing things Malcolm's way, or anyone else's way, I didn't feel his worry and wanting to escape was just because of that. I had never seen him so worried—not since we were in the Red and White Kingdom and he took me up in that tree. Something else was going on, but I wasn't sure what it was.

Deciding to push any thought of Chase to the back of my mind, I got ready for the day. Since I was just going to go around talking to people and checking out more houses, I decided to wear one of my floral dresses. After taking a quick shower and changing into my dress, I headed down toward the library where I figured the rest would be waiting.

As I ventured down the hall, I saw someone I didn't particularly want to see. I bit my lip as she headed over to me.

"Alice! You are back!" The Duchess hurried over as fast as she could in her boot heels and frilly purple dress that looked like something out of a production of a French aristocrat comedy.

"Duchess, great to see you in the morning."

She kissed my cheeks. "No, it is great to see you! What brings you to Wonderland?"

I shrugged. "You know, still searching for links for Morpheus."

"Have you all found anything?" she asked.

I shook my head. "No, not yet. Going to go talking to some more people, but so far it has all been dead ends."

"That is too bad. We need to figure out who was behind that strange man so we can bring him down once and for all, and Wonderland can be safe!"

"I agree."

"Well." She smiled. "I believe you will figure it out. You are too smart, Alice. I wish you all the luck."

She kissed my cheek once again and skipped down the hall. She was a strange one indeed, and I wondered why Chase hated her so much, other than she could be quite annoying. What sort of things did she make him do?

Shaking my head, I headed down the hall toward the library. As I entered, I found Melvin, Davis, and Malcolm all waiting. When he saw me, Malcolm furrowed his brows.

"Where's Chase?" he asked.

I shrugged. "Wasn't with me."

"That darn cat, I swear," Malcolm muttered. "He knew we needed him today. Whatever. Melvin and Davis can go with you, and I will stay here and go through some more papers. People know… that I would stay behind on missions, so it works."

So Chase had disappeared after coming to my room last night. I felt bad, as he seemed really frustrated, but he was asking too much of me and asking for me to do something I didn't want to do.

I hoped he was okay. Although it was kind of his fault, I still worried. Did he run off somewhere? Would he eventually come back? He wanted to run away, so what if he didn't come back? I felt my stomach start to wrench. What if I never saw him again? Just because I didn't have feelings for him didn't mean I wanted him out of my life.

"Report back here around dinner," Malcolm added, looking away from me. "And… maybe we can go to that ramen shop you all have been raving about."

I smiled. "Yes, let's all go there tonight. I would like that." I was glad that he was starting to come around. Maybe we could end on a better note before I left. Something felt like it clenched my heart. I shouldn't have thought about leaving, as this land was magical and had everything I had ever wanted. Why couldn't I have both? It just wasn't fair.

"Ready, Alice?" Davis asked as he saw me standing there, staring off.

I nodded. "Yup, let's go."

We headed out of the library. It would be strange to

have to actually have to travel, but since we weren't doing a real job and just killing time as Malcolm looked over notes, it was kind of nice. I got to enjoy the landscape and see all the different types of people that made up Wonderland. I looked forward to meeting new people here, as they were all kind, or at least mostly kind. More so than my world at least.

Melvin procured us a wagon and two horses and we all three sat at the front as he held the reins. I smiled as I peered out at the Dream Kingdom as we descended the hill and admired the rolling hills that led us to the closest two districts, which were the Garden District and Forest District. Beyond those two were the Mountain and Ice Districts. I wondered how far we were going to travel today and whether or not I should have brought thicker clothes. Hopefully we would stay in the warmer climate areas.

As we ventured farther through the hills, we came upon the forested area, and I remembered when I first came here and we had to hide from Bill. It felt like just yesterday my world turned upside down and I found out Wonderland was a real place. So much had happened though. I couldn't believe how much I had done here.

How much I could do.

I let out a sigh, and I could feel Melvin and Davis watching me, wondering what I was thinking. I tried not to appear melancholy, but I knew I was failing miserably.

"This would be easier if Chase didn't disappear," Melvin commented. "Where the heck could he have gone?"

I shrugged. I knew why he had left, but I couldn't tell them. Not only was it embarrassing, but I also didn't want them to give Chase too much grief. Not since I wouldn't be here much longer. Or would I? I still didn't know. Davis watched me as I seemed to ignore the question.

"Spill it, Alice. What happened?"

I was surprised by Davis's up-front question. Usually he wasn't like this.

I turned away. "I… um…"

Melvin intervened. "He made a move on you, didn't he?"

My face turned red—I could feel it. I knew it was obvious now, but I didn't know how to answer. That was not something I wanted to be discussing with them. "How did you—?"

"Because he's obvious about it." Davis sighed. "That stupid cat—what was he thinking?"

Melvin shook his head. "I'm going to straight up punch him, I swear."

I was fast to intervene. "No, it's not his fault. I mean, I understand why he did what he did…"

Davis raised an eyebrow. "Oh? Do you…?"

"No! I mean… Well, with everything that has happened with Malcolm, I don't know what to think. I care about Malcolm and wouldn't simply pick Chase because Malcolm broke up with me. I mean, if I chose either of them, I would have to live here, and I don't think I could live with myself if I made Malcolm see me with someone else. I love him…"

Melvin side-eyed me. "He loves you too, Alice. But he knows it was a mistake to have feelings for you when you aren't from here and need to go home after all this is over."

That wasn't something I wanted to hear. "But why? Why must I leave?"

"Do you want to stay, Alice?" Davis asked.

I hesitated. "I mean, yeah? But…"

"But you will be leaving your family and Kate behind," Melvin finished with a sigh.

I nodded. "But Chase said that they would forget I even existed. I guess it wouldn't be as horrible as completely disappearing on them. They wouldn't think I was kidnapped or lost or something. I mean, I wouldn't have left them like that either way. I would have told them where I was going… Not that they would believe me. But if I was going to disappear from their memories… That doesn't seem so wrong."

"This is true, but you will remember them forever, Alice," Davis said. "And that is where the pain lies. You won't die, and the years will go by. And what if you and Malcolm get in a big fight? You will have to deal with the pain you are feeling now forever. Or what if something happened to Malcolm? You would have to live centuries without him, and you will regret this life."

I never thought about it that way. What if something did happen to Malcolm? I mean, he definitely knew how to hold his own during a fight, but anything could happen—just like it had for Howard. Would I be able to keep going? It was one thing to only live a decade or two after a loved one passed but another to think about centuries going by.

And it was a feeling they all knew as the first Alice had already left them. Who knew how many other friends they had lost over time.

"I didn't think about it that way."

Davis placed his hand on my back. "We want you to stay, Alice, but it's not that easy. We don't want to talk you into something you don't want to do. It's why Malcolm has tried to stay away. He doesn't want to cause you to make the wrong decision."

I grabbed my head and started messing up my hair. "Ugh! This is so complicated!"

Davis and Malcolm nodded.

We traveled farther through the forest toward the Orchard District. I definitely was going to pick up some peaches and apples, as they had the best, which was saying something since I lived in Oregon.

"What are we looking for, or what are we acting like we are looking for?"

Melvin answered. "The man who disappeared here was named Bart Seitz. He wasn't one of Morpheus's people but died from whatever happened in your world. These people don't know that, however, so we can ask around."

I nodded. "Sounds good. And get some food?"

Davis was quick to comment. "Of course. Berries go well with cheese. And apples. And pears. And grapes."

Melvin sighed. "Everything goes well with cheese to you."

"That's because cheese is amazing."

I nodded in agreement. Hopefully there would be a place that sold fresh cheese as well so we could splurge on our fake mission.

CHAPTER FOURTEEN

It was just before evening when we got back to the library. Malcolm appeared as if he was ready to pull out his hair. The three of us entered slowly, trying not to interrupt his concentration. He glanced over and jumped a little, as he hadn't noticed us enter. Not many people entered the library since, well, they had been alive so long and already went through so many of these books. This place was more to keep records than to visit, although there were sometimes a few scattered visitors.

Malcolm pinched the bridge of his nose as we walked over, then rubbed his face. "Is it evening already?"

Melvin nodded. "Yup. You should probably call it a day. You don't want to work for too many hours, or you might miss something."

Malcolm looked like he wanted to flip the table but instead just slammed his fist down. "Okay. Fine. Where do you all want to go for dinner?"

I shrugged. "You mentioned earlier that you wanted to try that ramen place. If that still sounds good…"

He took a deep breath. "Right… We said that, didn't we? It has definitely been a long day."

"I-I can help, you know. I feel bad that you are here all alone," I commented and realized it sort of sounded like I wanted to be with him, which I did, so I didn't try to correct it.

Malcolm stretched his arms over his head. "It's not your fault. If Chase didn't decide to play hooky like he did, then Melvin and Davis could have stayed with me and helped. Stupid cat. I can't wait until I find him—he will wish he never showed his face again."

"So he never showed?" Melvin asked. I frowned. I had thought that he would have shown up by now. I wondered where he could be.

Malcolm shook his head. "Nope. Off doing gods know what. Every time I need him most, I swear…"

Melvin and Davis exchanged glances, and I gave

them a "you better not say a word" look. They listened, thankfully.

I turned back to Malcolm. "So, should we head out?"

He nodded. "Yeah, just give me a few minutes. I just need to finish up these last few pages. It's been a frustrating day."

I took a seat at the table, a little excited he was having a full conversation with me. I tried not to show it though, but I could tell Melvin and Davis were giving each other looks. They totally shipped us.

"What is frustrating you the most?" I asked.

He sighed. "I've been through everyone's signature who is still alive, and none of them match up. Whoever it is, either is really good or they aren't one of us."

That wasn't a good sign. There was no way that the note was fake, and it didn't seem like they knew it existed in the diary. They had gone to that house to destroy evidence that linked back to them for a reason, so there had to be a match somewhere here.

Malcolm shrugged with a smile and a wink. "I will figure it out though. They can't deter me forever."

His gesture made me smile. He used to make that smile and wink to me a lot, like he was flirting. Was he starting to open up to me again? Maybe he was realizing that I should stay here with him. No, it wasn't that. He just didn't want things to end on a bad note.

I glanced around the library. There had to be

something in here that answered who was behind this. As I peered around, I felt something calling me. The feeling was nostalgic, and I tried to remember when I had felt like this before. It reminded me of when the first Alice gave me the sphere to save Wonderland, but a lot less direct. I listened to it though, as it drew me to one of the books on the shelves. One of the books almost glowed, although I had a feeling it was my imagination. I pulled it out, and it appeared to be a romance novel, which made little sense to me. Why did it feel like something called me to this? Was I missing something? I examined it some more. It had a cute cover—one of a women in an old Victorian outfit with a little perfume bottle that was shaped in a heart.

Davis walked over to where I was. "What's that, Alice?"

I shrugged. "I don't know. I felt strange and pulled it out, thinking maybe the old Alice was giving me a clue, but it's just a romance book. Looks cute though."

"Maybe you should read it. Something might come from it. And if not, then you just get to enjoy a book."

I nodded. "Yeah, good point. I will go to the desk and check it out. I will be right back."

I went to the desk and quickly gave my info to the librarian. I signed the back slip and was told to bring it back in a week. It was easy enough. I met back up with the others, and we headed out for dinner.

The ramen place was still popular and crowded, but just like last time, we were able to get a table in the back. Malcolm still hadn't tried this place, as he decided not to join us the first time, so he took a little bit of time to look over the menu. He decided to go with the vegetarian ramen, and we all ordered. I also got the vegetarian ramen, which was a little awkward as ordering the same meal as someone else always felt like it was copying. It was a strong notion but one I noticed other people felt as well.

I glanced around, half expecting Chase to show up out of nowhere. He had been missing since last night, and I felt bad that I didn't listen to his plea to run away. It just didn't feel right, nor did I want to be put in that position. But I felt as if I were missing something and that there was more to just running away. What could it be though?

"Looking for Chase?" Malcolm asked as he took a drink of his tea.

I shrugged. "I suppose. It just isn't like him to disappear like this."

Malcolm laughed. "Oh, yes it is. You don't know him like we do. He used to disappear all the time. It was why no one trusted him for a long while. I had hoped that these foolish choices were behind him, but clearly I was wrong."

I wanted to stand up for Chase, but I didn't want to

start an argument with Malcolm, not to mention Chase did just disappear. I had explained part of it to Melvin and Davis but not about him wanting me to run away with him. If Malcolm found that out, he probably would beat Chase into a pulp. Not because he was jealous or anything, but because it would jeopardize Wonderland.

And that was what was important right now—Wonderland's safety. After that, I could worry about everything else and make my decision.

The ramen came, and we ate our delicious meal in silence. I wished it wasn't so awkward and meals were more like what they used to be at school and such. But that life had moved on, and this was as close as I was going to get to Malcolm. I honestly didn't blame him for being cold with everything he had dealt with in the past and because he didn't want me to make the wrong choice for him. It was rather sweet and was honestly making me want to stay even more.

We finished our meal and decided to head back to the palace. We would be doing pretty much the same things tomorrow, and I would have to search another area and fake question people all over again. Although I liked traveling, I couldn't help but feel that I was wasting time. I knew that wasn't technically true, as we needed a diversion, but it still sucked.

The four of us said good night to each other, and I decided to relax in my room and read the book I picked up. I hadn't ever read a fictional book of this world and was curious what they were like.

I changed into my pajamas, which was a light blue nightgown. I seriously wondered why these weren't a thing anymore in my world as they were very comfortable.

Settling on the lounge chair, I opened up the book and started reading. The first line, "A broken heart is better than solitude, as one knows they are capable of loving a person," captivated me. It was a bold statement for a book to begin with, and I had to know why this narrator, or character, thought that.

Hours passed as I kept reading this book. I couldn't put it down. I hadn't sat down and read a book for fun in a long time, other than manga of course. Most of the books I read were for Honors English, and they weren't as interesting as this. This book was a couple hundred years old though, and I wondered if I could write a report on it and turn it in as a classic. Probably not, since it technically didn't exist.

Before I shut the book, I scanned the last pages to learn about the author. It was actually a dream who wrote the book, and I wondered if the dream represented someone in my world that was an author, or if the dreams here had their own dreams, which made my brain hurt. I wanted to spin a top now, just to see. Before I set the books down, I glanced over the checkout list.

That was when it caught my eye—one of the signatures was the same handwriting as the note.

I could be wrong, of course. I was just basing the cursive style on what I remembered from the note. But if I was right, then I needed to act fast.

Running out of my room and toward Malcolm's room, I didn't stop and realized I was still in pajamas. It wasn't like he had never seen me in my pajamas, but I felt a bit awkward with the guards in the hallway looking at me as if I were crazy.

That didn't matter now—right now I needed to tell Malcolm what I found.

I knocked on Malcolm's door. He opened, looking a bit tired. He simply had some pajama bottoms, and I didn't know where to keep my gaze. His eyes, Alice, his eyes. I realized that it was probably the middle of the night now, as I had been reading the book for a while now.

"Alice, what is it?"

I held up the book. "This signature—tell me if I am wrong."

He studied it for a moment, then grabbed the book. "Come inside. I have the letter."

I followed him into his room. All the tables were littered with used teacups. I couldn't believe how many he had. Was this how he dealt with stress? It made sense, as he was the Mad Hatter.

He pulled the letter out from under one of the tea platters. Quite logical, if he was indeed hiding it and not that his room was just messy. I wondered how many were from just tonight or if he actually drank out of this many cups at once. I wasn't sure if I wanted to know the answer.

Malcolm sat down and studied the signatures.

"This is most definitely the same person. Bill will have to confirm, but if we are right, then we will have to make the arrest as soon as possible. I can't believe the person was under our noses this entire time."

I nodded as I glanced down at the Duchess's signature. She was the one behind it all.

CHAPTER FIFTEEN

Malcolm led us to Bill's room and pounded on the door. Bill opened it, rubbing his eyes. "You have any idea what time it is?"

"We think we figured out who is behind it all. Can we come in?"

Bill turned and yelled. "Kenny, put some clothes on!" He turned back to us. "He sleeps in the nude, as you know, Malcolm."

Malcolm sighed. "Even while camping."

I turned away and looked down the hallway to make

sure I wouldn't accidentally see him. That would be so awkward. After a few minutes, Bill opened the door all the way.

We stepped inside, and Malcolm laid the letter and book on the table. Bill studied the signature and compared it to the cursive writing that the letter had been in.

"Yeah, these are the same for sure. She had changed her normal handwriting in the past few centuries, or at least how she wrote any official letter. She must have slipped up when checking out this book. We can go confirm with letters from the Heart Kingdom era, but I don't think we will see a discrepancy."

Malcolm sighed. "Do you want to go arrest her or should I?"

Bill yawned. "I think we should both go, just in case. Alice, go with Kenny back to your room. He will keep guard until Malcolm is done. And Kenny, even if you are tired, no sleeping in the nude."

I blushed and hoped he would listen to Bill. I didn't argue though. I was used to being guarded by now. And I had a feeling Kenny wouldn't be stupid enough to undress in front of me. At least I hoped.

I turned to Malcolm. "Good luck."

He nodded. "Thank you. Now get back to your room. We don't know if she has anything planned for you yet, and I don't want to take my chances."

With that, Kenny and I headed down the hallways back to my room. On the way, I caught sight of a purple-haired boy with cat ears.

"Chase? Where have you been?"

He turned, probably surprised that I was out so late. "Alice, what's going on?"

I hesitated, so Kenny answered. "Duchess is getting arrested for being behind Morpheus's attacks." Kenny grabbed the back of Chase's neck. "And before you go to run off and help her…"

"Hey! I wasn't going to do that! I don't work for her anymore!"

"Sure… Well, then you won't mind coming to Alice's room with me."

Chase didn't answer but walked with us. He didn't meet my gaze, either because he was ashamed about all that happened last night or embarrassed Kenny was holding him like a mother cat to a kitten. I was surprised by Kenny's rashness and almost brute force. Usually he was laid-back and quite silly, which made me wonder more about Chase's past with the Duchess.

We got to my room, and all took a seat on the couch and a couple of chairs I had. I sat on the couch next to Chase, but neither of us said a word. I glanced down and clutched my pajamas, feeling a bit awkward that I was still in them.

"I'm going to go change…," I commented as I got up

and went into the closet. I shut the door and put on some loose simple clothes. Stepping out, I found Chase and Kenny looking away from each other.

"What's wrong?" I asked.

Both shook their heads. "Nothing."

"Okay…" They totally argued about something, but it must have been in whispers as I hadn't heard anything while I changed in my closet.

"What happened while I was gone?" Chase asked. "How did you figure out it was the Duchess this late at night?"

I took a seat next to him on the couch. "I picked up a book at the library. It felt like it was calling me. Call me crazy, but I think the spirit of the original Alice directed me to the right book. Well, I read it all because it was quite good, but when I looked in the back, I found her signature when she checked it out, and it matched the handwriting on the note we found."

Chase nodded. "That is crazy."

I shrugged. "But Bill and Malcolm agreed; it matches. They are going to check her old handwritten notes, but they are making the arrest now."

Kenny glanced over to Chase. "Question is, why didn't *you* recognize the handwriting?"

Chase folded his arms. "Because I don't memorize every single person's handwriting in Wonderland. Besides, it's been decades upon decades. It's not something I would remember."

Kenny rolled his eyes. "As if. She sent you letters all the time."

"You all have received letters as well from her. Why didn't any of you remember?"

Kenny and Chase held each other's glare. I had never seen Kenny this angry at anyone. Granted, I wasn't around when he worked for the Heart Kingdom, but even when he went off about the tarts, he didn't seem this angry.

I held up my hand. "It's no one's fault, and we eventually figured it out. Chase isn't to blame when he has been helping us for almost two years now, if not more."

Everyone was silent now. I let out a sigh as I leaned back and closed my eyes. "I think I'm just going to pass out on this chair now, if you don't mind. It has been a long day." To be honest, I just wanted to be less awkward, and the only way to do that was sleep.

"Good night Alice," Chase whispered.

Both Kenny and Chase were silent as I tried to fall asleep. I could almost feel their tension, however, as I leaned back and tried to get some sleep. As I was about to realize I could have just gotten up and slept in my bed, the darkness took me in and I passed out.

When I woke, sunlight was filtering through my room. I

found that I was still on the couch but was leaning against Chase. I quickly moved away, a little flustered. I hadn't meant to fall asleep on him but must have leaned over. Chase didn't move but had his head tilted down. He was out still. I was glad, as I didn't want to be more awkward about this incident.

Glancing around, I found Kenny at the door. I craned my neck to find that he was talking to Malcolm. Malcolm's eyes drifted to me and then to Chase, who sat next to me. My cheeks went red, but there was really nothing I could do. He turned back to Kenny, and they went on talking.

"So she's been arrested?" Kenny asked with relief in his voice.

Chase's ear twitched, which told me he was now awake and listening in to their conversation. I couldn't blame him, as I was too.

"Yup. She didn't put up much of a fight but is claiming to be innocent. We are going to go to her main estate later and look for any more evidence. I have a feeling we will find something." Malcolm turned to me. "Alice, I'm glad you are all right. I hope you slept well as we have a lot of work too. You too, cat. I know you are awake and listening."

Chase got up and shot Malcolm a look. Malcolm shrugged.

"I know you too well. Also, don't think you are going

to get off easily after the stunt you pulled yesterday. But it will have to be after the trial, as I need your full support."

"Looking forward to it."

They glared at each other some more. I coughed. "Well, let me change into something easier to work in, and then I will meet you all outside."

I grabbed a blue button-up shirt, a white vest, and beige pants to wear. It was similar to the first outfit I wore while fighting Morpheus, so I figured it was fitting to wear it on the last mission I would ever have. I changed into the clothing and looked at myself in the mirror. I couldn't believe this was the end. So much had happened—so many laughs and cries and struggles. I knew that wasn't the point of this mission and that I shouldn't be worrying about it finishing when Wonderland was at stake, but I couldn't help it. I didn't want to leave.

Shaking away those thoughts, I went to meet the others outside my door, grabbing my katana along the way. One didn't know if something was going to go terribly wrong. I found all three of them standing outside my door, with Malcolm and Kenny glaring at Chase.

"Uh," I commented. "Ready when you are."

Malcolm nodded. "Well then, Chase, after we grab the others, will you transport us to the Duchess's mansion? Unless you have a reason not to."

Chase shook his head. "Doesn't matter to me. I don't have any loyalty to her."

Malcolm narrowed his eyes. "Right. No loyalty. I will keep that in mind."

I wondered why they were all so suspicious of Chase. I mean, I understood that he once worked for the Duchess, but that was a long time ago. It seemed that everyone had changed since that time, and yet they still held him with suspicion. No one expected Malcolm still worked for the Heart Queen and such. I knew she was gone from this world, but it was still the same point. So why was Chase suspected for working with the Duchess?

We reached the meeting room we typically used to meet in together. Melvin, Davis, and Bill were already there, going over some details it seemed. As I entered, I found a blueprint of the home laid out on the counter. The three of them stared at Chase, either in suspicion or because they were surprised he was now with us. I wasn't sure which one it was.

"Chase…" Davis was the first to speak. "Where the heck have you been?"

Chase rolled his eyes. "None of your business, pipsqueak."

Melvin held back Davis as he was about to punch Chase but still gave him an icy glare. "You know,

Chase, there is a reason you aren't trusted around here, and it's because of comments like that. You disappear when we need you most—you pull stupid stunts and cause problems, but we always welcome you back. Do you see why we are a bit frustrated?"

Chase laughed. "Welcome me back? You lot have never been welcoming to me. You have been suspicious of me for so long, even though I have helped this Kingdom time and time again. If I was working for the Duchess, do you think I would be here? I could easily break her out right now and disappear, but have I? No, because my loyalty lies with the Dream Kingdom."

Everyone was silent. He had a point. There were plenty of times where he could have sabotaged things, but he hadn't. He was also the one who helped me find the note. If he wanted to, he would have accidentally destroyed it or something.

I stepped forward. "Chase is right. We need to put our differences aside and finish this. If he was going to betray you all, he would have already done it. I think there are a lot of things you all have gone through, and you all have your views on each other because of that. But for this, we need to look past all that and end it once and for all. Then we can celebrate and perhaps get into different arguments."

"Alice is right." Malcolm sighed. "As much as I want to blame Chase for everything, the fact still stands if he was going to betray us, he would have already done it. Now, Chase, will you transport us there? Then we will split up and search through the entire house."

Chase nodded. "Right. Let's go."

In an instant, Chase teleported us to the Duchess's mansion. I gasped at its wonder, curious why she would leave it to stay at the palace most of the time. It was huge, like something out of French aristocracy. The building was made of a white stone, which contrasted the large bushes that had been cut away to make different animals line the front. The windows were all sparkly clean and the lawn freshly mowed.

Why was this not the palace? It was actually larger, at least on the outside. This was crazy.

"Impressed?" Malcolm asked as he saw my face.

I shrugged. "It just wasn't something I was expecting. It's so huge."

Malcolm chuckled. "I suppose you are right. The Duchess always kissed up to whoever was in charge at the time, so she grew quite a bit of wealth."

"I can see that."

"But as you can see, it is quite large, which is why we are all here. We will need to break up into groups of two again." He glanced over at me. "Would you mind being on a team with me?"

My face turned red. Was he really asking me that, after months of trying to push me away? I glanced around and everyone was staring, as if thinking the same things as I.

"Sure…"

He smiled. "Thank you." He turned to the others. "Melvin and Chase are a team, and Kenny and Bill are a team. We will check the upstairs, Melvin's team the main level and Bill the basement. Davis, there should still be some servants working on keeping everything neat and tidy. Look for them all and have them gather in the kitchen, then keep an eye on them until we are done so we can bring them all in for questioning. Does anyone have any questions?"

Everyone shook their head, and we were on our way. We passed by the bushes that had been cut so delicately.

Although I had seen some bushes that had been cut into shapes, I had never seen so many that were perfectly shaped like this. It had to be hard to keep up with, and I couldn't imagine working with plants as an art medium. Maybe someday I could try my hand at it, but I barely could even do pottery.

I shook my head. Why did my mind always move to art? Why couldn't I be like a normal person and focus on the task at hand... in Wonderland... Okay, so perhaps what I was doing already wasn't a normal-person thing, but my point still stood. I needed to focus.

We entered the building, and I gasped at the entryway. It was everything I had ever wanted, if I were royalty. I mean, it wasn't like I was going to try to have a house like this, but a girl could dream, especially one who grew up watching Disney movies. There in the middle was a grand staircase with marble statues on each side of the Duchess. The floor was also marble, and I felt as if I was going to accidentally break something. Or slip. Or both.

"Chase, you used to live here?" I commented, as we hadn't split up yet. "It's so amazing."

He shrugged. "I wouldn't call it living. Besides, I didn't stay here for long periods of time as I was always on some kind of mission. And we stay in a palace now, Alice, and also stayed in a castle in the Red and White Kingdom. This isn't anything *that* special."

That was a good point, but this place was still amazing compared to anywhere else in Wonderland. The Dream Palace was grand, yes, but this was different. It was more expensive and felt larger. Then again, I didn't know the Heart Kingdom before it was in ruins, so perhaps it wasn't as grand compared to that.

Malcolm grabbed my hand. "Let's go look upstairs."

I nodded. Feeling his warm skin on my own made my heart race. I missed him and the comfort he gave me. I still didn't quite understand why he was giving me this affection now, as this was our last mission. Did he find out about Chase kissing me and realized he still had feelings for me? Or was he just trying to make Chase mad? I glanced over to Chase and saw him frowning before he turned away and walked off with Melvin. Kenny and Bill headed down the hallway, which I presumed led to stairs that went down into the basement.

I was glad Malcolm and I weren't searching the basement this time, as being trapped in the basement of the Heart Kingdom had left me being afraid of any underground floor. Kate had a basement, and even though I had been in it a million times, now it gave me the creeps. It was where their Ping-Pong and pool table was as well, which was a shame because I loved playing those games. Now I usually said I didn't like playing much any longer and we did something else.

Stupid basements.

We made our way upstairs, and this whole setup reminded me a bit of *Clue*, as each team had to search a different floor. As we made it to the upper level, I found that doors lined the hallway each way I looked. I sighed as I realized this was going to take a long while. Malcolm saw my look of worry as there were so many rooms, and he laughed a little.

"I figured we could start with the doors on the left and then come back for the other side of the hallway, then go search the other side of stairs. I know her room is on this level, but I am unsure which door and whether or not we will find what we are looking for. We will be able to search them all, don't worry. We just have to have a method down so we don't double our workload."

I nodded, blushing a little as I had seemed so overwhelmed. "That sounds like a plan to me."

The first door we opened was a bedroom, but it appeared more like a spare bedroom than what would be her main one. We searched through and found nothing of concern, as it hadn't seemed like someone had been in there for months. There was no dust, however, as the maids must have kept it clean.

Searching the next two rooms, it was much the same. I couldn't believe that there were so many bedrooms, but I supposed it made sense if she had company constantly when she lived here.

When we went into the fourth room, we found that it was quite used and that the maids seemed to have ignored it. There were clothes scattered on the floor and laid out on the bed, a half-lit candle on the bedside table, and dust covered the dresser. Malcolm bent down and picked up one of the shirts.

"Whose room do you think this is?" I asked.

Malcolm shook his head. "I have no idea. Most of the people in Wonderland all wear the same type of clothes, otherwise maybe we would know whose room this was. It seems to have not been touched for a while, as if the maids just ignored it. Whoever it was didn't like other people going through their stuff."

We searched through it all, but whoever this person was didn't leave much behind, other than clothes. I opened a drawer of the bedside table to find a piece of paper. I quickly read it and found that it was indeed a clue.

"Malcolm, whoever this person was, worked closely with the Duchess. This piece of paper says to let her know the moment Alice was found."

I handed the paper to him, and he quickly read it. "And this handwriting matches that of the one you found. It doesn't make it clear that it is the Duchess though. We will bring it with us since it does show that someone here was looking for you."

"Does that mean someone else is working with the

Duchess?"

"It does. So don't tell anyone we found it, okay? It could be anyone at this point…"

I nodded. I couldn't believe anyone we worked with would be in with the Duchess, especially after her arrest, but I wouldn't go against Malcolm's wishes. He knew this world better than I did about Wonderland.

But did this mean he actually thought it could be Chase?

I glanced at the clothes again. They didn't seem ones that Chase wore, but they were his size. Then again, Melvin and Malcolm were also the same size, so that didn't say much. Chase wouldn't betray us though. Not after everything we had been through.

We left the room and searched the last couple of rooms on this side of the hallway. Both of them were clean, just like the first few. It was apparently just the one room that hadn't been touched for a while, which made it all the more suspicious.

Making our way across to the other side of the mansion, going through the plain rooms and bathrooms along the way, I hoped the others were doing better in their searches. Although we had found the note, it wasn't anything incriminating. We entered the first door on the right. The room was clearly a study as paper lined the entire area. Both of us sighed as we knew it was going to take us a lot of time to get through. I shouldn't have wished we would find something on our end.

"Well… I guess we should get on it…," I commented as I started glancing over the papers. Malcolm joined and stood next to me. I felt myself blush as I could feel the heat of his skin. He skimmed a few of the pages that lay on his desk. So far it was just notes to friends and nothing incriminating.

I noticed Malcolm kept glancing up at me. I tried to ignore it, but then I thought maybe there was something on my face.

"Is there something wrong? Do I have food on my face?"

He laughed. "No, nothing like that, Alice. I just… I wanted to apologize."

I furrowed my eyebrows. "For what?"

"For the past few months. It wasn't gentlemanlike to treat you like I have. I just… I didn't want you to leave everything behind for me, and so I tried to push you away. But in the past couple of days, I realized how wrong I was to do that, and I missed being around you. For that, I am sorry."

I bit my lip. So Melvin and Davis were right; he still cared for me. "The past couple of days have been nice. And I'm sorry I put you in a position like that."

He shook his head. "You did nothing wrong. It was all me."

"Thank you for apologizing, and I forgive you. I understand why. I still don't know my choice, but I feel I will make up my mind soon."

"And I will honor whatever you choose, even if it is the wrong choice."

I rolled my eyes, and we both laughed but were happy that we were finally on the same page. As we went through more of the papers, I found something that stood out. I reread it again and again and couldn't believe what it said… and whose name was on it.

"Umm… Malcolm?" I whispered.

"What is it?" he asked as he set his papers down.

I handed him the piece of paper, and he read through it. I could tell he did the same thing as I did, rereading it to make sure he didn't miss anything. He let out a deep breath. "Damn him."

"You weren't supposed to find that."

We both turned to find Chase standing in the doorway, frowning.

CHAPTER SEVENTEEN

"And you were supposed to have me search the top floor so I could destroy them," Chase added.

Malcolm stepped in front of me. "You stupid, stupid cat. After that whole story of how you moved on—after telling us that she doesn't control you and that you would never hurt Wonderland. You played us. You lied again and again to get close to Alice."

"I never wanted to hurt Alice. I just—"

Malcolm shook his head. "No, you were after her this whole time. It finally makes sense—why everything you seemed to do went wrong. It never was an accident, the times she got captured by Bill in the Red and White Kingdom and by Morpheus. It was you."

Chase was silent. Had he really been working for her all that time? I thought back on all the time we'd spent together. Was it all lies? Had it all been to get close to me for the Duchess?

Malcolm went on, "I should have known. I shouldn't have listened to Howard—I should have banned you from joining us. But now he said I need to learn empathy and to forgive as people changed. But you clearly didn't change! Clearly my suspicion was always on point and I need to trust my gut!"

He shook his head. "You don't understand. I can't disobey her! Every time I have tried to run away— every time I think I am free of her, she calls me back! I have no control of my actions! It's like she has an invisible collar around my throat, and when she needs me, she just yanks it! Anytime I have ever tried to run away, it grows tight and I can't breathe!"

That was why he wanted to run away—he was trying to escape all this. I felt bad, but I didn't know what to do at this point. I tried to step toward him, but Malcolm held out his hand. "I will not let you near Alice. You know as well as I that those were lies. You could have told us—we could have helped to break the spell she has over you. But instead, you lied and told us you broke it yourself. This is why no one will ever trust the Cheshire cat."

Chase's eyes turned red. "Whatever, it doesn't matter now."

With that, Chase disappeared.

I stared at where he once stood, still not believing everything had just happened. He couldn't be the traitor. He had done so much with us—he was the one who found the note. He was the one who kissed me and told me he wanted to be with me.

How could he have done this to us?

My knees buckled, and I fell to the ground, confused and distraught. Was this why he wanted me to run away with him? Did he want to run away from her? Or was he going to take me to her? Were his feelings for me real, or was he faking it?

Malcolm knelt down beside me. "Alice, are you okay?"

I shook my head. "No. He was my friend. How could he do this? How could he betray us?"

"He is the Duchess's cat. She has some kind of spell over him. I have been suspicious for a while, but I didn't believe he would go this far."

"He said he couldn't control it—like she had some kind of spell on him. We could help him… We can do something, right?"

I took in deep breaths, trying to calm myself down.

Malcolm patted my back.

"Alice, it is important we go check on the others. We also need to sweep this room to see if there are any other letters, but I don't want to leave you here alone in case he comes back and takes you to the Duchess. Can you walk?"

I nodded as I stood up. Everything around me felt like it was a blur, and I just wanted to curl up in a ball. Chase had betrayed me, and now I had to fight him. This was crazy.

But was it really against his choice? Could he not disobey her? And if that was the case, could we do something to help him? It didn't seem like Malcolm wanted to try to help him—as if all that Chase did was his choice—but if I knew anything about magic from all my manga, it was that sometimes one didn't have a choice. Spells could be powerful like that.

We ventured down the stairs and went toward the kitchen where Davis was waiting with some of the butlers and maids. They all appeared to be confused about what was going on. I doubt any of them had anything to do with what the Duchess, and Chase, were doing. As we joined Davis, Melvin came running into the kitchen.

"Malcolm, Chase ran off!" Melvin exclaimed.

Malcolm nodded. "I know. We found evidence of his involvement. He came upstairs and then confronted me, then he disappeared. I'm not sure where he would have gone, but we will need to alert the palace. Can one of you go find Kenny and Bill so they can run to the palace, and the other one of you help me finish searching the study?"

Melvin nodded. "I will help you search. Davis go find the others. And take these servants with you for questioning."

Davis ran off toward the staircase, and the rest of us went back upstairs. I took a seat on the green velvet couch and held my head in my hands. Melvin and Malcolm discussed something, but I couldn't concentrate enough to understand what they were saying. I couldn't believe all this was happening. Why would he do this to us? Why was this happening?

I tried to go through everything that happened since I met Chase. Malcolm accused everything that went wrong when we first defeated the circus had been his trying to sabotage it for the Duchess. Was that true? The notes went over how he was supposed to report when he had found me… but why wait this long? Why wait until after Morpheus was stopped when they could have captured me a long time ago. What was their end game?

There were probably a lot more steps in this plan than we could have ever imagined.

"What is this for?" I asked as I stood up and started pacing. Malcolm and Melvin had been flipping through the pages that lay on the desk. They already seemed to have a pile of things they were going to take in form. "What do they have to gain? What do they want?"

Malcolm and Melvin glanced at each other. Malcolm answered, "Alice, sit back down."

So they were finally going to tell me the truth. I plopped back down on the couch.

Malcolm knelt down in front of me. "Alice, I didn't want to have to tell you about your full potential because, well, I didn't want to scare you and because I had hoped you wouldn't ever have to use it. The Dream Kingdom is quite fair, and we don't want it to change. But the truth still stands—you have a power within you that can change everything about Wonderland. Remember the orb you used at the circus? The one you thought you destroyed?"

I nodded. "Yes."

"Well, it's not really destroyed. It's something that is inside you, and if you called upon it again, you can fulfill any wish. When you destroyed it the first time, your wish was to restore Wonderland. Well, if I had to guess, the Duchess wants you to use it to make her become the Queen of Wonderland."

Although it was a lot to take in, everything started to make sense. It was what Morpheus had told me—that I was important. It made sense that they didn't want anything to really change, like for the Heart Kingdom and the Red and White Kingdom, but they still could have told me. What if I had accidentally used it wishing for a land of ice cream or something? But all this still didn't explain Chase's involvement. "But this isn't like Chase. How could he help her?"

Malcolm shrugged. "I don't think he gave it much thought in the beginning. He probably was promised his freedom, but then when we found you, he started to have a conscience and kept postponing the inevitable. The Duchess should have made a move earlier, and my guess is that he kept disobeying her with little things. However, we started to find clues, and he had to finally show himself."

If that was the case, I wanted to help him—I wanted my friend back.

Melvin interjected. "It makes sense now—all the things he did in the beginning like tell Alice we weren't going to the circus, taking her up to the tree during the fight. He might not even have made a bunch of portals so that we would be found."

Malcolm nodded in agreement, as he had already come to that conclusion.

I shook my head. "I don't know what to think anymore. This is a lot to happen in a day."

Malcolm sat down next to me. "And that is okay. We understand. We will take the papers we have found to the King and Queen and they will figure out the

Duchess's punishment. Then we will search for Chase and try to work with him, okay? As long as he comes willingly."

The question was, however, would he come willingly? Or was he going to fight us? And what would Malcolm and the others do to him if that were the case? I recalled how he reacted to Morpheus in the Dark Forest. He had killed him in cold blood. Would he do the same to his own friends? Did he ever consider Chase an actual friend?

I nodded. "Fine. But promise me you won't hurt him…"

Malcolm made a small smile. "Oh, Alice, you are always so nice. Don't worry, we won't hurt him, but we might have to knock him out. Don't forget, he can travel anywhere in an instant. He has never been easy to catch. But we will try our hardest. I promise."

"Thank you…"

Melvin kind of rolled his eyes but didn't say anything. His rabbit ears twitched a little. "Malcolm, I think we should get out of here, just in case Chase comes back with reinforcements, although by now I'm not sure that any are sided with her any longer. My guess is that if she had some spies, they have abandoned her side to save their own skin. It is just Chase we will have to look for."

He nodded. "Right. We will have to scour the

Kingdom for him. I don't know what backup plans they had in place, but if I know Chase, it won't be anything pretty. Alice, you stay by my side and hold my hand this entire time, okay? That way if Chase pops out of nowhere, he can't transport you without transporting me. You understand?"

"Yeah…" I grabbed his hand, and we started off toward the entrance to this enormous mansion. We would have to walk all the way back to the Dream Kingdom, and I just hoped it wasn't too far away as all the adrenaline and surprises the day brought made me extra tired, but I knew I wouldn't be able to sleep until all this was figured out.

CHAPTER EIGHTEEN

"How far is the palace?" I asked after about thirty minutes of walking. Clearly the Duchess's home was not close to the palace.

Malcolm sighed. "About two hours if we simply walk. I am hoping that we will run into someone with a wagon and we can ask them to take us there. That will cut our time tremendously."

I hoped for it as well, as I did not want to walk for another two hours. I searched the hills we traveled over for any signs for a wagon, but thus far there was nothing. I let out a breath.

Glancing down at our hands, I smiled a little as Malcolm and I had been holding hands for the past half an hour. I had to admit, I missed being with him like this; granted that it was so I couldn't be abducted. I still couldn't believe that Chase had done all this, and I wished he didn't disappear but just sat down and talked with us. Then again, he had technically committed treason, so I didn't quite blame him for running. I just hoped he wouldn't do something stupid.

"So what all did you find in those papers?"

Malcolm and Melvin glanced to each other. Clearly it wasn't anything good. Malcolm simply smiled. "We will go over them at the trial…"

"No, Malcolm. Tell me what's on them. I deserve to know. I'm already knee-deep in this anyway…"

He let out a breath. "Fine. They were details on everything Chase and Morpheus had done and their plans on what to do with you. It seems originally Morpheus was to overtake your mind and get you to use the orb to change Wonderland, which you did, but it was supposed to be for the Duchess. Then you were supposed to be captured by him last year when he was hiding in the Heart Kingdom… And it was Chase who transported you there every time. I'm not sure how he was able to do it in your dreams, but his connection was the one that made it possible."

I gulped. So it really had been this entire time—Chase had really been using me.

"Then he was supposed to take you to her after Morpheus died. It seems he had put that off for too long, and their plan foiled."

"At least he tried to stop it then?" I commented. "I mean… He could have finished this a long time ago."

"He has that going for him, yes. But right now that is it. He still worked to take over the Kingdom and claims the Duchess is controlling him."

"What if we make the Duchess take her spell off him? What about then?" I asked.

Melvin shook his head, causing his rabbit ears to sort of flop all over. "It's not that easy. She would have to admit she was guilty, and that is likely not going to happen."

"Oh…"

Malcolm squeezed my hand. "But you are right. He didn't take you to the Duchess when he could have, so he has that going for him. It seems he hasn't made his move."

Melvin and I exchanged glances. He did make a move in a different way though, and now I wondered if it was because he wanted to save me from her or get me to go along to her. Malcolm noticed our glances and frowned. "What didn't you two tell me?"

My face went red. Crap, I didn't want to tell Malcolm

what had happened. "I… um… Chase… Chase kissed me."

Malcolm's face went cold. "He did *what*?"

I held up my free hand, trying to calm him down. "I pushed him away! For the record… I mean… I know we aren't a couple, but I am just saying I didn't want to be with him. I think he just… I don't know…"

"Was going behind my back?" Malcolm handed Melvin the papers. "Can you hold these for a moment?"

Melvin took them, and then Malcolm grabbed his head with his free hand. "That insolent cat!"

I thought about trying to calm him down, but there really wasn't anything I could say that would stop this. Chase had gone behind his back—Chase had tried to make a move on a girl he still cared about and was trying to not have ties to this place.

That, or he was trying to get me to go to the Duchess. I still wasn't sure.

Without thinking, I leaned in and kissed Malcolm's cheek. I didn't know what came over me, but I just felt it would help the situation. He stared at me, surprised I would do such a thing.

"I… Sorry…" I blushed and looked away.

Malcolm turned my face to his and leaned in and kissed me. I missed his lips and smiled after he backed away. He smiled as well and squeezed my hand.

Melvin coughed. "Uh, we need to get going…"

"Right." Malcolm retrieved the papers back from him. "Any sign of a wagon?"

"Actually, while you two were making out, I saw something move in the distance. I think we might be in luck."

Malcolm nodded ahead. "Run up and see if you can catch up with them. We will be shortly behind."

Melvin nodded and started running toward what he had seen in the distance. I prayed he was able to catch up to them while Malcolm and I strolled along the road. I felt a bit bad he had to run, but I also really didn't want to.

He was able to reach the man in the wagon, and we all hopped in back, which was rather hard to do without letting go of each other's hands. We traveled along toward the capital, which ended up being only an hour instead of two.

Once there, everyone seemed to be in the streets and around the palace, waiting to see what the decision would be for the Duchess. Apparently, the whole Kingdom already knew she had been arrested, even though it had only happened that morning. I watched as they gathered and yelled out to the guards to give them answers. It seemed the Duchess had a lot of fans. We moved past everyone and made it inside.

"Those people all like her?" I asked as we were out of earshot.

Malcolm nodded. "Unfortunately she can sweet talk them all. I'm sure you have politicians who are like that on Earth."

That was for sure. "What's the plan now?"

Malcolm handed the papers to Melvin. "Melvin is going to take these to Bill and the King and Queen, and you and I are going to wait in the meeting room until the trial is ready."

I nodded and we went toward the meeting room. No one was inside, as I figured Kenny and Davis were watching the Duchess to make sure Chase didn't do anything, and Bill was with the King and Queen. I took a seat with Malcolm.

"Do you think there is enough evidence to put the Duchess away?"

Malcolm nodded. "There is definitely enough. I just am not sure what they are going to do to Chase. Hopefully he shows up so he can prove he isn't guilty, but thus far he isn't showing his innocence."

I prayed that he did, and he wouldn't do anything stupid. Unfortunately, however, we were talking about Chase, and it seemed like he always caused problems.

As I sat there, I realized something important.

"Uh, Malcolm?"

"What is it?"

"I… I kinda need to go to the bathroom. But we are holding hands."

He frowned. "It's not safe to stop holding hands."

"How about this? If Chase tries to teleport in the bathroom to kidnap me, I will personally kill him."

Malcolm laughed. "That's fair. Okay, it should be fine. I couldn't see him trying something like that anyway. He has some class, even if it is just a tiny bit."

Malcolm walked me over to the bathroom down the hall and stayed right outside so he could take my hand after I was done. Once I was finished, we went back to the meeting room and waited to be called upon by the others. After about an hour, Bill finally stepped in.

"The trial is ready."

We both nodded and followed Bill through the halls. I had never been to a trial and wondered if they were the same or different from the ones in my world. We did have that mini trial for when Malcolm killed Morpheus, but I had a feeling this would be much different.

As we entered, I found the King and Queen sitting where the judge normally would sit. Bill went up and at their side next to the White Rabbit. We went over to the side where Melvin and Davis were already seated. Many dreams from the Kingdom lined the room, shouting and arguing. The Duchess was in a cage in the middle of the open area in front of the King and Queen for everyone to see. She looked like a caged bird as she was still wearing a giant, colorful dress.

That part of the trial was a bit different.

"Now we may begin," the King began. "Duchess Thalia Duncan, you are on trial for conspiring to overthrow the crown, destroying the citizens of Wonderland, and using Alice for your own benefit. How do you plead?"

"Not guilty, Your Honor," the Duchess lied in a sweet songlike voice. The crowd went wild, saying this was unjust. The King slammed down the hammer and everyone went quiet.

"Very well," the King turned to us. "Malcolm, will you begin?"

Malcolm stood up and spoke out to the crowd next to me, as he still had my hand. "Your Majesty, I have found from the original Morpheus a letter that matches the Duchess's handwriting, along with notes to conspire against the Kingdom. These all match her handwriting during the Heart Kingdom era, which shows she has been conspiring and waiting for decades for the next Alice.

"On top of this, her pet cat, Chase, admitted to his involvement and to being under her control. Unfortunately, he has disappeared, but after this trial we are going to send out search parties."

The King nodded. "Thank you, Malcolm. May I see the notes?"

Malcolm nodded to Melvin, who pulled out the papers from his suit pocket and brought them up to the

King. He and the Queen read through them.

"These are indeed the same handwriting. Duchess, how do you plead now?"

The Duchess's lips curved in a sadistic smile. It was a complete contrast to her normal sweet smile. I didn't think someone like her was capable of such a one eighty, but apparently, I was wrong.

"Fine, I will admit, it was me. It's not like if I said no that you will listen. All you care about is your precious Alice. Only Alice can change these lands, but what if the lands aren't changed for the better? It seems to me that Wonderland is just destroying itself, hoping Alice will come along and fix it. Well, I'm sick of it! I'm sick of being ignored! I'm sick of this land not recognizing my importance!"

So, this was her true nature. I could see why Chase was afraid of her.

"I want to create a Wonderland that will last forever —I wanted Alice to make me Queen! I can lead this world to something great, but I have always been ignored!"

The King and Queen whispered to each other, and then the Queen finally nodded. The King turned back to the Duchess. "Duchess Thalia Duncan, you are sentenced to execution. With Chase on the loose, it will be expedited. You will be beheaded within the hour."

Everyone gasped, and I couldn't believe what I was

hearing. Beheaded? That was still a thing? I turned to Malcolm, who seemed to be levelheaded and not reacting to any of this. Was this normal? I supposed it was as he used to be the executioner. Would Malcolm have to execute her?

And if the Duchess was beheaded, would Chase finally be free?

CHAPTER NINETEEN

This was the worst thing to wait around for. Even worse than a final.

I mean, we were literally preparing to kill someone. I didn't even think I could comprehend what we were about to do. Not to mention these people were practically immortal, so the death sentence felt even more extreme. But she did seem like she wasn't going to change, and with Chase still out there, a possibility of escape was very high since she was controlling him.

On one side, I was happy that her death might make

it so Chase would be free, but at the same time it would mean someone's death. I glanced at all the others. None of them seemed to care that we were waiting to execute the Duchess. Was this normal to them? Could I ever find this normal if I lived here? I didn't want it to be.

One downside of Wonderland—it was a lot more violent at times.

My world could definitely be violent, however. Perhaps my world was actually more violent, and I had just grown up somewhere safe. I sighed, as now I wasn't sure if that one negative point counted. I hadn't come up with any downside to Wonderland other than my parents and Kate not being here. But was it right to pick Wonderland?

Malcolm squeezed my hand. "Don't worry—this will all be over soon, and you will be safe."

I smiled. "Yeah, I suppose. Will you… I mean… Are you still the executioner?"

Malcolm's eyes went sad for a moment, but he simply shook his head. "No, I don't have to. The White Rabbit is going to do the honors. He also used to be an executioner and a very thorough one at that."

I could believe that, as he tried to kill me when we first met. It still gave me shivers thinking about it. I didn't like being around him that often. I guess that was one negative thing about Wonderland, but it wasn't that bad as he stayed with the King and Queen mostly.

Malcolm and I were still holding hands, which got to be a little weird after so many hours. We switched which hand it was, as sometimes my hand got sweaty. I also found that I used both hands while I talked a lot more than I thought I did. I kept yanking on his hand and felt bad about it.

I looked over at Melvin and Davis, who had been pretty quiet as we waited for Bill and Kenny to set everything up. It didn't seem there was much to do, and I wondered where exactly it all would take place. Would it be like a hanging in the olden days when it was done in front of everyone?

"Why do so many people like the Duchess?" I asked. "I mean, she's pretty and all that, but I can't see why…"

"Why people would want to follow someone so abusive and manipulative?" Malcolm asked. Davis let out a laugh.

Melvin answered. "Because she can sweet talk anyone. We are used to it—we know how she really is. You are taken aback by her because you aren't from this world and aren't used to the politics here. You also are persuaded by the popular kids at school, which is practically what she is."

He had a point. She did remind me of a cheerleader. Now I would never unsee her with pom-poms.

"So she's just popular because she's cute and has

charm?"

They all nodded.

"Huh. Maybe I should learn how to sweet talk…," I mumbled to myself.

Malcolm shook his head. "Please don't. I don't want to date a popular girl."

The room was silent. Date? Were we dating again? He realized after a moment what he said. "I mean… Not date, but umm. I just don't want you to be known like that by anyone."

I nodded, blushing a little. "Right."

Davis was smiling a little. He definitely wanted us to still be a couple. I did as well, but with everything going on, I didn't think it was a good time to bring up my decision on staying. It could wait until after it was all over.

The hour passed, and the execution was to commence. Malcolm led us outside to the front of the palace where a man with an ax awaited.

There was no way I could watch this.

I had seen Malcolm kill Morpheus, but that was a lot different than watching someone's head get cut off. Besides, I didn't know Malcolm was going to do that at the time, and if I had known, I probably wouldn't have stayed around to watch.

I glanced over to Malcolm, who didn't seem fazed by all this, which made sense since he used to be the executioner in Wonderland. Was this what he dealt with constantly? Morpheus had said he lived in the Dark Forest, so I doubted there would be an audience. Was that better or worse?

Guards held back the angry mobs of citizens who refused to believe the Duchess was guilty. She literally confessed though and said why she committed treason. She wanted to become Queen. I couldn't blame her, as she had seen the rise and fall of at least three different Kingdoms. The Duchess probably believed she knew how to run a Kingdom that would never fall, although I had a feeling that was far from the truth. She just wanted more eyes on her and more power to do what she wanted, at least that was what I gathered from the others.

The Duchess didn't seem worried as she stood in front of the crowd, her hands bound behind her by cuffs. Her face was calm and collected, and she even had a bit of a smile on her face. I didn't understand how she wasn't afraid of what was going to happen. If I were her, I would have been crying and pleading for my life, but she kept a calm presence.

Which made me believe something was going to happen.

Bill kept his hand around her arm, making sure Chase didn't appear and take her away. It was why they sped up this entire process, after all, as Chase seemed to be a wild card in this mess. I missed him, even though it had only been hours. I just hoped he was safe and that this would help.

The King unrolled a piece of paper. "I, King Bartholomew the III of the Dream Kingdom, hereby sentence Duchess Thalia Duncan to death for conspiracy to destroy the Kingdom for her own gain, kidnapping Alice, and the death of many citizens by Morpheus. Do you have any last words?"

"Yes I do, if I may. You all think this is over? Far from it."

I felt Malcolm stiffen. He didn't like how this was going either. It seemed as if she had something up her puffy sleeves.

The Duchess turned to me and smiled. "I will survive, and Alice, dear Alice, you will come to me, begging me to help you."

The crowd went wild, demanding she be free. The guards were able to hold them back, but the chaos of noise added to the foreboding feeling I knew each of us had. I glanced around, seeing if I could spot Chase anywhere, sort of like when Captain Jack was on trial in *Pirates of the Caribbean*, but I didn't see him anywhere.

"Quiet!" The King yelled out to the crowd. "Order!"

Most of the people became silent, as they respected the King, but some still lashed out. As everything began to calm down, we noticed a figure on the balcony above the entrance.

It was Chase.

He had two things with him—one, the Looking Glass, and the other was a person who appeared frightened as her eyes were wide, confused, and distraught. I couldn't believe my eyes.

"Kate?" I gasped. "Chase, what are you doing?"

Chase stared at me, as if trying to say he was sorry, but instead gave his demands. "Release the Duchess, Bill, or else I will kill this human!"

"You dirty good-for-nothing cat!" Malcolm shouted. "After everything, this is what you are going to pull! You know what happens if you bring a human here!"

My heart tightened as I remembered when I first traveled to Wonderland. Malcolm had said if I hadn't been the Alice they were looking for, I would die. Was Kate in danger? Would she be all right?

"Chase! Please! Let her go!"

He shook his head. "Not until you let the Duchess go."

"Alice." Kate's eyes were wide, and she was wearing her usual pajama shirt and shorts. It was still nighttime in my world. "What's going on?"

Tears were forming in my eyes. "Don't worry. I will help you, okay?"

"Bill! Step away from her right now!"

Bill glared at Chase, but he knew he had to do as she said for a girl that was once his student. He let go of the Duchess, and in an instant, Chase teleported down, grabbed her, and teleported back to the balcony.

The Duchess smiled as she stepped forward. "Now, Alice, I have one itty-bitty request. You have twenty-four hours to meet me at my mansion and use your powers to give me Wonderland. If you do not come, Kate will cease to exist."

Tears ran down my face. No, this wasn't happening. There was no way this was happening. I stared at Kate, who still appeared in shock. It was the same look when I first stumbled upon this place. She looked like she wanted to run, but Chase kept a hand on her.

Why was he doing this? Why didn't he let the Duchess die so he could be free? He had made his move, and now there was no way that the King and Queen were going to pardon him. He had brought a human here—he had a hostage. A hostage I cared about. How could he do this?

I had to save her. I couldn't let anything from this world affect her like this.

I started to step forward when Malcolm pulled me back as we were still holding hands. "No, you don't."

"What do you mean? Kate needs me!" I pleaded. "Let me help her! I need to help her!"

"I won't let you destroy Wonderland."

I turned to find Malcolm's eyes dark. He had sworn to protect this Kingdom. If I went with the Duchess, then the entire world would be destroyed and under her rule. It would probably be a cruel one—something like the Heart Kingdom. She would be all powerful, and it would be nearly impossible to stop her.

But I couldn't let my friend die for a world she knew nothing about. It wasn't fair. I had to do something.

"Please, Malcolm…"

He shook his head. "No. We will figure something out. But you aren't going with her."

The Duchess laughed, making both of us turn our attention back toward her. "Well, I guess I will make my escape. Remember, Alice, you have one day to come to us. If we see anyone else near my estate, we will kill her." She grinned. "And we have the only means to travel out of Wonderland, so Alice will be stuck here forever either way. The clock is ticking. Make your decision."

With that, Chase and the Duchess disappeared with Kate and the Looking Glass.

CHAPTER TWENTY

I couldn't believe what had just happened. Chase completely betrayed us. It wasn't just him having originally been a spy—it wasn't him trying to sabotage our plans—he had gone to my world and kidnapped my best friend. He was willing to kill her to get what he wanted. He didn't even try to let the Duchess die. He didn't try to get her to stop controlling him.

Kate appeared horrified. She didn't know anything about this world, and yet she was stuck in the middle and was being threatened with her life. I couldn't imagine what she was going through at that moment, and I wished I could have gone with her to tell her it was all right. She didn't deserve this—she didn't deserve any of this.

I had to help her—I had to go and save her before it was too late. They had said twenty-four hours before she would disappear. That was doable, right? I could go and rescue her and she would be safe. The only problem was that the Duchess wanted Wonderland, which wasn't something I wanted to do. I couldn't betray Wonderland, but I also couldn't let Kate die.

What was I going to do?

I watched as Bill began to push buttons on the device that he had strapped to his wrist. I had completely forgotten that he could open portals back up. I broke free of Malcolm's grip and ran over to him.

I grabbed Bill's arm. "Don't! If you go, she might kill my best friend!"

Bill tried to pull away from my childish clinging. "Alice, the Duchess wants to destroy Wonderland. We can't let her escape. It is my duty to stop her."

"But we know where she is going. They said they are going back to the mansion, so we can figure something out. Please, she can't die!"

Bill glanced over to Malcolm, who was now stepping up to us.

Malcolm sighed. "Alice has a point—we should do

what we can to save Kate. We will come up with a plan to get the Looking Glass, Kate, and take down the Duchess. If you give me a few hours, I think I can come up with something."

I nodded, glad to have someone on my side. He knew the importance of a life. He wouldn't let my best friend die. "Thank you."

He took my hand. "That being said, I don't think I can do all that with you wandering about."

I narrowed my eyes. "What do you mean?"

"I mean… You are going to be stuck in your room for a bit. With Kenny."

I shook my head. "No, I'm not going to sit around and do nothing when my best friend is in danger! There's no way! You have to let me help!"

"I'm not going to let you make a foolish decision and destroy Wonderland. If push comes to shove, you might not like what we will have to do or what we will have to sacrifice. I will do everything I can to keep her safe, but my loyalty to Wonderland and the Dream Kingdom comes first. We can try to put together a plan and save Kate, capture the Duchess and Chase, and get the mirror back, but I can't promise anything. So, I need you to wait in your room until all this is over, so I don't have to worry."

So, he was still willing to put her life in danger is what he was saying. I did not like hearing that. I tried to pull my hand away, but Malcolm was being serious. "Malcolm, please! I have to help her!"

"You are a liability. I know she is your best friend, and if I were in your position, I'd probably make the same stupid decision. But I'm not, and I have to save my country."

"You don't understand! I can't lose someone I care about for this world! I just can't!"

His eyes turned cold. "You think I don't know what it is like to lose someone I care about for the good of this world?"

I had forgotten. Howard. He died in battle to save Wonderland—he died in battle to save me. I didn't know how many others had died in the line of duty next to him. How many friends had he lost? What would it be like to live hundreds of years and watch as your friends died?

What if Kate died and I would have to deal with that same pain?

I didn't want to think about it, but that was childish in this instance. I had to think about it—I had to figure out what I was going to do or else something bad might happen. The question was, did I trust Malcolm or would I have to intervene?

"I'm sorry… I didn't mean…," I began. "She's just my best friend and doesn't deserve this."

Malcolm wrapped his arms around me. "I know. And

I will do everything in my power to bring her back. But I need you to promise me you won't do anything stupid."

I nodded. "I promise."

The King stepped forward. "Malcolm, I heard you said you are going to work on a plan to stop the Duchess. Please let us know if you need anything."

Malcolm nodded. "Of course, Your Majesty. I will do everything I need to do to keep this Kingdom safe."

"Just as you did when the circus had done everything it could to stop us. Even when we were under its control, you still were able to keep this Kingdom safe. I trust you and believe you will bring the Duchess to safety. We give you permission to use any means necessary and to bring her back dead or alive. You will not face repercussions if you dispose of her."

"I understand."

"As for Chase, we would like him alive but know the difficulty in capturing him. Use your talent to secure safety against him as well. He is now wanted for treason, unless he has physical proof he had been under the Duchess's control. As it stands, I deem him guilty."

"Of course."

Chase… I couldn't believe what he was doing. Had all this been his plan from the start? I just couldn't believe it. How could he turn his back on us like that? And to put Kate in danger? Did the Duchess tell him to do that? To use someone close to me as collateral? She didn't know me—she didn't know what went on in my world. Chase had to make that decision on his own, and I wouldn't forgive him for that.

The King left us, and Malcolm turned to me. "Are you all right?"

I shook my head. "No, and I'm not sure if I will be. My best friend was just captured by my other friend. It is a lot to process."

"We all feel betrayed by him, don't forget that. He made his choice, and he will face those consequences. For now, do you think you will be okay without me? As I need to start planning the attack so we can reach the Duchess in time."

I slowly nodded. "Yeah, I think I will be all right for the time being.

"Good. Now let's get you back to your room, and you can get some rest. We have a long day ahead of us."

I doubted I was going to be able to rest, but I nodded, and they led me back into the palace as the King and Queen were led by the White Rabbit, just in case Chase came back to do something to them. It seemed unlikely as the Duchess was truly after me.

Kenny followed behind, but he wasn't his normal playful self but was serious as he was concerned for the safety of Kate and the Kingdom as well. This was going to be the longest twenty-four hours of my life.

We got to my room, and Malcolm let me go. "Don't worry, Alice, once we figure something out, I will come get you once we are finished. I will save Kate, okay? Trust me."

I nodded my head, but I didn't know what to think any longer. My best friend had been kidnapped. She didn't understand this world—she couldn't survive this world. What was I going to even tell her? Oh yeah, this is where I hang out…

Malcolm shut the door behind him, essentially locking it. I glanced around the familiar room—the room I was usually happy to be in and excited to start adventures the next day. It was the same room Chase kissed me, Malcolm held me close, and where I found that I could truly be myself. Now it appeared like a prison where I would have to wait to find out whether or not my best friend had survived whatever plan Malcolm came up with. I held myself tightly and let out a sigh. Not even my plush Eevee could comfort me now.

Kenny took a seat. "So, Alice, what do you want to do to kill time?"

I shrugged, not liking how he phrased that. "I don't think I can focus on anything right now."

"Don't worry. Malcolm is the best fighter in the world. If he says he will save your friend, he will. There is nothing to worry about."

"Then why is he locking me in here?"

"Because you would run off and do what the Duchess asks to save your friend. You have a loyal heart. Also, we don't know what the Duchess will do to you once she uses you, so he wants to keep you safe."

I took a deep breath and let it out slowly. "I don't know what to do, Kenny. What would I choose if I had to? I can't let my friend die, but I also can't betray Wonderland like the Duchess wants me to. What is the right choice?"

Tears began to fall down my eyes. Kenny stood up and held me tight.

"There is no right choice—that's the problem. Malcolm knows this as well, and that is why he is doing what he needs to. Then you won't have to make the choice."

I nodded, sniffling. "What happens if we don't save her within twenty-four hours?"

Kenny hesitated. "She disappears in this world and yours. All her family and friends will forget she even existed."

"Except me, right?"

"Yeah, except you. It is the same if you decided to stay here. All your family and friends will forget you, except you can survive this world."

"So I've heard."

"But as you can see, there are a lot of people who

want to use you to take over Wonderland. This is another reason Malcolm didn't want you to stay—you would constantly be in danger. Even if we execute the Duchess, there will be some other power-hungry lunatic wanting your powers."

"Because someone will always want the throne."

"Yup."

Now I really didn't know what to do. Right now, though, I would have to focus on Kate and doing whatever it took to get her back to our world. I didn't care what price I needed to pay—I couldn't let her die.

Which was why Malcolm locked me in here—he knew I was willing to give the Duchess what she wanted. Was it wrong though? Would the Duchess be a bad ruler?

I checked the time. We had a little more than twenty-three hours to save her. It was at least a two-hour journey there on horse. I would watch the time, and if I hadn't heard from Malcolm when the clock showed three hours left, I would take matters into my own hands.

CHAPTER TWENTY-ONE

I didn't get any sleep. Surprise. Although I hadn't slept in over twenty-four hours, I had been used to pulling all-nighters when I would stay up to paint, then realize I had forgotten to do my homework, not to mention fear had pumped so much adrenaline in my body that I wouldn't be able to sleep for quite some time.

To pass the time, Kenny and I played different board games and card games. Currently we were playing Kings in the Corners. It was a fun game and not one I had played since I was little when my grandma was visiting. We were on our twentieth game, and I still couldn't believe that Kenny was down to one card. How was he so good at these games? He had won over three-quarters of them. It wasn't fair. Although my mind was somewhere else, I shouldn't have been losing this many times.

I placed down a five of clubs over the six of hearts. "Your turn."

He pulled a card, then smiled. "I win!" He placed down a four of diamonds and a three of clubs.

I threw my remaining five cards on the table and rolled my eyes. "You are too good at this."

"I know. It's because we used to play these games all the time when we were in the Heart Kingdom. We had to always let the Queen win, however, but the rest of us played for reals. Bill is really good at games, and so is Malcolm."

I could see that as they were experts in strategy. Speaking of which, I glanced at the clock. There were less than four hours left, and we hadn't heard a peep.

"Don't worry, they are probably executing the plan as we speak." Kenny noticed my worry.

I shook my head. "He said he would come and tell me the plan. I have a bad feeling about it all."

"No, I think he was going to report back here after everything was finished. I wouldn't worry about it. Malcolm is the most talented fighter in all the

Kingdom."

"I can't stop worrying, Kenny. They have my best friend, and she has been in their hands for twenty hours. She doesn't know anything about this land, and I doubt the Duchess would tell her what's really going on."

"No, but Chase might. I doubt he would leave her cold and dry. He probably gave her some information."

While that made me feel a little better, I frowned. Chase had stabbed me in the back. After everything we had been through, he still did this. We went to class together, went to dance together, and told each other everything. He read my manga and watched anime with me, yet he still…

I shook my head. There was no point of thinking about it now. He made his decision even if he was supposedly forced. He could have asked us to help, but instead he tried to do it all alone, and it meant he stabbed us in the back. I wouldn't forgive him even if he begged.

"If we don't hear from them soon, what then? There will only be a few hours left before we can save Kate. I don't think I can just sit here—"

"But we are going to sit here because this is what Malcolm wants. He wants you out of the way. If you want this all to succeed, Alice, then you need to sit still and wait it out. He will save her, I promise."

"Pinky swear?"

He tilted his head. "What?"

"It's a saying in my world. Pinky swear. It's like swearing on your parents' grave but a lot less morbid. Hold up your pinky."

Kenny held up his pinky, and I grabbed it with my own. "See, you do this and it means you can't break your promise."

"Huh. Your world has strange customs."

"That we do. But I think this one is rather cute. Kate and I pinky swear all the time."

I took my hand back and sighed at the thought of her. Kenny noticed my shift in mood.

"What do you two promise each other?"

I shrugged, not sure if going over some of our promises would make me feel better or worse. "Oh, you know, girly things. Like that we will keep each other's secrets, that we will always split a donut if there is only one left, that we will still talk to each other in college…" Tears started forming in my eyes. "That we will always be friends."

"Alice, I'm sorry. I shouldn't have asked."

I shook my head. "No, it's fine. I like talking about her. Besides, she's not gone and Malcolm is going to save her."

Kenny nodded. "Exactly. Malcolm always saves the day."

I smiled a little. That he did, but as I watched the

clock keep ticking, I began to worry. What if he couldn't save her? What if he wasn't coming here to tell me the plan because it was going to be risky and he couldn't guarantee her safety?

"Want to play another round of Kings in the Corner?" Kenny asked as he shuffled the card. I glanced at the clock. A little more than three hours remained. That's how much time it would take to go over and save her if I needed to intervene.

What if they won't succeed? What if they already tried and didn't succeed? My heart was constantly racing now, and I felt as if I were going to pass out.

I needed to get out of here. I needed to do something.

But how? It wasn't like Kenny was going to let me simply walk out of here. No way I could beat Kenny in combat. I wouldn't be able to hurt a friend, and he was also a lot stronger than me.

That didn't mean I wasn't going to find some way out of here.

Glancing around, I realized the best way to sneak out was to break through the paper walls. Only problem was, how would I do that without Kenny noticing? I couldn't get far when he was using the restroom since he made me talk the entire time so he could hear me.

But what if I cut my way out through my closet?

I wasn't sure if that was possible, but it would be my only way I could get out and get distance between us before he figured I ran for it. Girls were notorious for taking a while to change, right?

Not all girls, of course. Any girl who went through ballet learned to change fast, especially during a performance. But Kenny didn't know that. I checked the clock again.

This was my only chance.

"Alice? Another game?" Kenny repeated. I had completely forgotten he had asked me. I yawned and stretched.

"I'm getting tired. Do you care if I go change into some pajamas? Maybe I can get a little nap in before Malcolm gets back."

He raised an eyebrow. "You are tired now? You don't peg me as someone who could sleep with all this going on."

He had a point. This entire time I had been refusing to go to sleep because of Kate, but now I was saying the opposite. I bit my lip.

"It has been a long couple of days, and my adrenaline has finally worn out. I could literally pass out soon."

Kenny studied me for a moment, then nodded. He must have figured there would be no harm in it. "Sure, go ahead."

"Thanks. I will be right back."

I went into the closet and shut the door. I literally had a minute. I grabbed my katana I had and poked a few places in the wall. Maybe I was wrong in how I thought the walls worked here when finally, part of the wall budged. I was right—it was similar to classic Japanese walls. I sliced open a hole big enough for me to sneak through, and I found that it went into a closet. I opened the closet to find that no one was in their room. It appeared to have been occupied, as there had been clothes, but I honestly had no idea who I kind of lived next to. I would apologize for ruining their closet later.

Opening the door to the hallway, I found that there wasn't anyone out there. Kenny hadn't noticed my escape yet, but I didn't know how long he would wait for me to change before actually opening the door. I hurried as fast as I could, without anyone noticing something was off and trying to stay clear of any guard who would know I wasn't supposed to be out of my room.

I carefully peered around the corners of the hallways, but it seemed most of the guards were either with Malcolm or the King and Queen. I was able to make it through the front entry without any problem.

Now I would just need to find a horse.

I was glad Melvin and Davis taught me how to ride a horse. I would have been screwed otherwise. I went over to the stable that most of the palace used and smiled to the guard.

"Hi, I need a horse."

The guard nodded. "Yes, Alice, of course."

I was thankful he hadn't been informed of everything going on and that Malcolm hadn't used all the horses on whatever mission he had developed. I was also thankful for the fact that since I was Alice and everyone recognized me, I could get most things I wanted. I didn't abuse this power, of course, but I did take note of it.

I waited for the man and noted that quite a few horses were missing out of the stables. So Malcolm had already started the mission, and I would need to keep an eye out for him. I didn't want to sabotage his mission, but I also wanted to make sure my best friend was all right. If all else failed, I would stay out of the way, and no one would even know I was there. If all went wrong, well… Then I would do whatever I could to save my best friend.

The man was taking a bit of time to retrieve the horse. I kept glancing up toward the palace, waiting for Kenny to appear and yell to stop me. That, or he had actually thought it took this long for me to change. Who knew with him?

Finally he was able to bring the horse and helped me put the saddle on and climb up on it. I took a deep breath and tried to remember which direction we had come from just a day before and set off toward the Duchess's mansion.

CHAPTER TWENTY-TWO

The horse galloped in the direction the Duchess awaited. I wished I brought a watch as I had no idea how much time had passed. This horse was moving faster than the wagon we had earlier, which made it in two hours. The only thing I had to worry about was the fact we had to stop every once in a while, for the horse to get some water, and it always took me a bit to get back on as I had no help. Luckily the horse was easy to work with, and I didn't have to worry about it trying to run away or trying to kick me.

The sun was getting closer to the horizon, and I wished for once that I did Girl Scouts when I was little. They learned how to tell the time from the sun, right? And stuff about the wilderness? Or was that Boy Scouts? Either way, I wish I learned more outdoor skills growing up. People didn't realize how important it was until it was too late and you were stuck, galloping on a horse through Wonderland, hoping your best friend was still safe.

So far I hadn't spotted Malcolm or the others, which meant they were closer to the mansion than I thought they were. What if they had already confronted the Duchess? What if the Duchess had already murdered my friend? I shook my head as I traveled farther down the road. I couldn't think like that—she had to be alive. She just had to be.

Once we came close to the estate, I started to slow down and kept an eye out for Malcolm and the others. I stopped my horse and tied him to a tree so I could sneak up on foot. I still wasn't sure what I was going to do, but I knew if I went in there without a plan or did something to jeopardize Malcolm's plan, it could lead to Kate's death. I couldn't let that happen. So, I decided I would sneak around and figure out what was going on first.

I snuck through the woods and came upon the garden that surrounded the back side of the estate. I hadn't seen it earlier when we were there since we stayed inside, but it was huge and had a maze similar to the Heart Kingdom's. The hedges weren't dead, however, and only came up to one's waist. I liked these a bit better but only because I was a little afraid of mazes after being attacked in one and not able to see what was going on. I had so many fears after coming to Wonderland—fears that made people wonder what was wrong with me in my world.

As I snuck up to the gardens, I realized how beautiful this garden was. The Duchess, although evil and vindictive, had style. I could imagine a lot of great parties here, if the owner wasn't such a *b*. I could imagine a scene like one out of *The Great Gatsby* happening here. I wondered what would happen to it after all was said and done. Would it become a wasteland like the Heart Kingdom and the Red and White Kingdom? Or would someone take it over, like Malcolm?

As I wandered through the gardens, staying out of sight from all the windows, I listened for anyone I could hear. So far, I hadn't heard anything. I decided the best plan of action would be to completely go around the building and look out for any signs of the others before making my choice on whether or not I should go in. Since I hadn't seen Malcolm nor the others between here and the palace, they had to be around here somewhere.

I went around the statues of the Duchess, as there were many, and the hedges that were cut out to look like her. The more I went through the garden, the more I realized she really did only care about herself. It was crazy to see so much art based only on one's self. Did she not have a favorite animal? Or anything? I sighed as I passed a sculpture that had water coming out of her mouth, like the fountains on Earth with baby angels. I wasn't sure which was weirder, as I always found the baby angels to be strange, but so was having one made of yourself.

I went around to the front gardens and began to hear voices. I stepped slowly and peered around a hedge, trying to see if I could figure out who it was. As I kept moving, I was able to make out who was talking.

The first voice I heard was Malcolm's. "It doesn't have to be this way. If you hand over the girl, I will guarantee that you won't get hurt. I will secure a place for you to live and never be bothered by anyone in the Kingdom."

The Duchess laughed, the high pitch hurting my ears. "As if I would believe you, Malcolm. You are this land's executioner. Once you have the girl, you will just kill me."

Malcolm didn't respond because honestly that was probably the correct answer. I doubted they would let her go free after everything she had done, even if she let Kate go.

"What would make you trust me? All I want is Alice's friend back. You know as well as I if she stays here any longer, she will disappear."

The Duchess laughed again. "Well, since you went against my conditions already, I don't think anything you say will ever make me believe you. And time is ticking, Mad Hatter. Bring me Alice, or the girl dies."

My heart was racing. I couldn't let Kate die—I couldn't let her life disappear because of me. I wouldn't be able to live with myself, whether it be in Wonderland or Earth.

"I won't bring you Alice. Just let the girl go."

"I promised to kill the girl if you showed up to my estate. I have been lenient, you know, hoping Alice will still show up. Perhaps I should just kill the girl right now."

I stepped out of my hiding spot. "No! Don't!"

Everyone was silent. The Duchess was smiling, which made me wonder if she knew I was there. If that was the case, why didn't she just say so? Did she just want to prove to Malcolm that she had all the cards and that he should just back down?

Malcolm's eyes widened, then he pinched the bridge of his nose. "That is the last time I have Kenny watch over you."

"Well… yeah. To be fair, how I snuck out would have tricked all of you. It was pretty clever."

"You went through the closet," Malcolm guessed.

I nodded. "Yeah… I did."

He shook his head. "I wouldn't have let you go in the closet. I know how all those rooms were built. Kenny should have known better as well."

I shrugged. "Sorry. I am here now though."

"And you will cost Wonderland its freedom."

I shook my head as Melvin, Davis, and Bill all watched Malcolm and I agree. "No, I am saving my friend. All of you would have done the exact same thing."

"Alice…," Davis began, but the Duchess coughed. We all turned back to her, and I gulped.

The Duchess smiled. "Alice. It is nice to see you again. I had a feeling you would show up sooner or later. And I have been generous, given that these men showed up and I didn't go through with hurting your friend."

I stepped forward. "Where is she? Take me to her. I won't do anything you ask until I see her."

Malcolm shook his head. "Alice, don't! You can't risk Wonderland because of some human!"

I whipped my head toward him. "Some human? She is my best friend! I can't let her die without doing something!"

Malcolm took a deep breath. "You leave me with no choice." He pulled out his sword and pointed it at me. "I will use force to stop you; don't think I won't."

I couldn't believe what I was hearing. Use force? Was he going to fight me? I didn't like the idea of fighting Malcolm, but I also knew I couldn't just leave Kate to fend for herself.

But I couldn't destroy Wonderland.

Would Wonderland really be terrible in the Duchess's hands though? It wasn't like she wanted to destroy it but more wanted it all under her control. She had served the Kings and Queens throughout the ages, so it made perfect sense for her to rule. She might be nice and know what to do.

And Kate's death wouldn't bring anything but torture.

Before Malcolm could do anything—before I could even think straight and figure out what I was going to do—Chase appeared and grabbed me. I screamed as I was in his grasp. Moments later I found myself in the hallway inside the mansion.

"Chase! What the heck?"

"I'm sorry, Alice… about everything. I didn't." He ruffled his hair and shook his head. "It doesn't matter."

He pushed me back into the room we stood outside, and I heard the door lock behind him. I started pounding on it. "Chase! Let me out of here!"

"Alice?" a voice said.

I turned to find Kate standing there, her eyes red, but at least now she was in a change of clothes that weren't her pajamas. She wore a loose button-up shirt and trousers. My guess was that they were Chase's.

Running to her, I wrapped my arms around her. "I'm so sorry this is happening. This is all my fault."

"But this is all just a dream, right? Wonderland isn't real. It can't be."

"Right." I smiled. "Just a dream. It will soon be over, I promise."

Suddenly Chase and the Duchess appeared in the room, as Chase had transported her from outside where she had been talking to Malcolm. I started to nod my head.

"Tell me what I need to do and promise me Kate will go free."

I held Kate close, not wanting her to feel scared any longer as the Duchess explained what I needed to do.

"It is really simple, Alice. All I need you to do is to give me the power you have in your heart. Once that is done, I can transform Wonderland into whatever I want. It is really easy. Remember when you called upon it in the circus? You do the same thing, except instead of breaking the orb, you hand it to me."

That seemed doable. I glanced over to Chase, who didn't seem to want to make eye contact with me. I understood why, as he had betrayed me and all the others. I wished there was a way I could help him, but I had a feeling that would have to be for another day.

"Alice… what is going on?" Kate whispered. "What does this woman want?"

"It's all right, Kate. You will be fine and forget any of this is happening. It's just a dream, okay?"

She nodded and held me. I took a deep breath and closed my eyes. I thought back to when I first used the orb to defeat Morpheus. That had been so long ago—could I still find the orb?

As I tried to clear my mind, going back to where I had met Alice, I found that it was harder than people made it sound.

I opened my eyes again. "I don't think I can do it. I need more time."

The Duchess shrugged. "You only have twenty minutes before your friend disappears. I can't really do anything about that. Not to mention your boyfriend is out there trying to break into my house, and if he succeeds and comes in here, I will have to end her life even before that."

I shook my head. "No, you can take Kate back, and then you, me, and Chase can go somewhere else and finish this. I will keep my word."

"I have had many people disappoint me, Alice. I am not going to make the same mistake again. Now, finish this up or you will have to say goodbye."

I closed my eyes and tried my hardest to focus. I could do it—I had done it earlier when it mattered most, and I would do it again when it mattered most. I had to or else Kate would pay the price.

Suddenly I felt my consciousness shift—as if I were transported somewhere different. I opened my eyes to find myself no longer in the Duchess's study but in the middle of the Dark Forest. Small blue lights hovered around just like it had the night I found what I needed to do for this.

In front of me was me, but younger, about the age of seven or so. She wore a blue dress and held the orb in her hands.

"You can't do this," the girl in front of me insisted as she held the orb tighter. "I won't allow it."

"But you are me and you know that I must save Kate. She is our best friend."

The younger version of me shook her head. "You can't sacrifice Wonderland."

"I'm not sacrificing Wonderland. Once Kate is safe, I will be able to stop the Duchess. But if Kate disappears, there won't be any way to bring her back."

"But what if you can't save Wonderland?"

I was silent. I hadn't thought that far ahead. I didn't want to think of that outcome. If Wonderland couldn't be saved after what I was about to do, I deserved to be charged with treason as well. "But sacrificing Kate might not bring the Duchess down. What if she dies but then tricks us anyway and still takes over Wonderland? Kate will have died for nothing?"

"But what if it does?"

I shrugged. "There is no way to know the outcome. But I know what I need to do in my heart."

The little girl frowned. "Fine, but don't say I didn't warn you." She handed me the orb.

Blinking my eyes open, I was suddenly back in front of the Duchess. The orb was now in front of me, and it lit up the entire room. The Duchess smiled, and I could hear banging on the door leading to the hallway. The others had finally made their way inside.

"Alice! Don't do it! She will ruin Wonderland!" Malcolm yelled from the other side of the door.

"Oh, dear Hatter," the Duchess said, although I doubted Malcolm could hear. "It is too late."

The Duchess stepped forward and took the orb, looking it over with such delight. The light bounced off her eyes, making them appear as if they were glowing.

"Now send Kate back!" I exclaimed. She nodded to Chase, who started to step forward to take Kate back to our world.

And that is when Kate suddenly disappeared into nothing right in front of me. I stared at where she once stood, confused as to why Chase was still here.

"What… what happened?" I whispered.

Chase's eyes became wide. He opened his mouth, but nothing came out. I just stared at him and where she should have been. This couldn't be happening—it just couldn't.

Her time had run out. Kate had disappeared in both this world and mine.

"No!" I screamed.

I collapsed to the ground, tears filling my eyes. There was no way she could be gone, was there? I had done everything I was supposed to—she should have survived.

No, this was a dream. This couldn't be real. I had destroyed Wonderland, and I had let my friend die.

Chase reached out to me. "Alice, I'm sorry. Please, I didn't want her to die. I didn't realize the time—"

I smacked his arm away. This was his fault—if he had just told us the truth, we could have helped him and saved Wonderland. Now Kate was dead because of him.

"You have no right to apologize to me! You betrayed me! You killed Kate! This is all your fault!" I exclaimed.

"Alice, please…"

"No! You can't try to apologize for this! I will never

forgive you!"

Chase backed away as the Duchess cackled.

"Finally! Wonderland is mine!" she exclaimed as she held up the orb. Suddenly everything around us began to change, as if morphing into whatever she wanted. Pieces of wood and stone flew through the air. It almost looked like something out of *Harry Potter* as magic flew through the air and reworked whatever objects were around into what they needed to be. If I wasn't still in shock, I would have marveled at it.

As the walls began to fall apart and rearrange themselves, Malcolm leaped inside the room and grabbed me.

"We are getting out of here!"

I didn't respond as he picked me up and carried me in his arms. He ran toward the large glass window, and just as it began to reconfigure, he leaped through it. I still expected to hit the glass, but there was nothing.

"Alice, please tell me your horse is nearby."

I pointed toward the tree I had tied him up at. "Over there. He should still be there."

"We have to get to him before she changes everything. There is only one place we can go where she can't touch us. Otherwise, we will be her servants and won't be able to resist."

Just like Chase. I felt bad telling him I blamed him, as it was out of his control, but if he hadn't gone and kidnapped Kate, none of this would have happened. He could have done something.

Malcolm made it to the horse, and we quickly mounted and sped through the woods, heading to wherever Malcolm wanted us to. I held on tight as he was pushing the horse as hard as he could. I peered back to find everything quickly changing, as if it were rearranging into some strange configuration. We had to hurry.

"Where are we going?" I asked.

"The Dark Forest. It is the only place that won't change no matter what happens. It's the only place Alice cannot change."

Great, that was all I wanted—to be in the Dark Forest.

"What about the others?"

He didn't say anything but kept pressing forward. I had a feeling that meant it was too late for them. I held Malcolm tight.

"I'm sorry. I just wanted to help my friend."

"I understand, as long as you understand why I tried to stop you."

"I do. Especially now."

He nodded and we kept moving forward. I kept glancing back to find the reconfiguration still on our tails. We wouldn't be able to stop for even a second.

I could see the Dark Forest in the distance. I took a

deep breath of relief even though I didn't particularly want to go inside.

"We are going to have to jump off the horse and make a run for it. The horse will be okay with the reconfiguration, but we need to get out before we are caught under its spell."

"Okay."

It made sense, as the horse would not be able to survive the Dark Forest. When it was time, Malcolm and I both leaped off the horse and ran into the forest, watching as the entire surrounding area changed.

This was it—we were the only two left in Wonderland who could save it.

<u>THANK YOU FOR READING</u>

Thank you so much for reading! Readers like you make it possible for authors like me to write stories! If you could spare a moment and leave a review on Amazon, Goodreads, BookBub, and wherever you like to buy books, that would mean the world to me! It really helps authors like me to succeed in the publishing world.

Acknowledgements

I want to thank everyone who made this novel possible.
A thank you to Annie at Victory Editing for helping
with this project and to Tamara for helping me with
content edits. Thank you to Biserka Designs for the
amazing covers they have done for my books. And
lastly, thank you to my husband and parents who are
always supporting me.

I also want to say thank you to Becca at Tippy Toe
Dance studio for letting me use you and your studio in
my book! And a thank you to Scott and Maria at Escape
Fiction for letting me include you in my book as well!
My high school years were amazing because of all three
of you, and I am glad I got to include it in this series!

About the Author

Dani Hoots is a science fiction, fantasy, romance, and young adult author who loves anything with a story. She has a B.S. in Anthropology, a Masters of Urban and Environmental Planning, a Certificate in Novel Writing from Arizona State University, and a BS in Herbal Science from Bastyr University.

Currently she is working on a YA urban fantasy series called Daughter of Hades, a YA urban fantasy series called The Wonderland Chronicles, a historic fantasy vampire series called A World of Vampires, and a YA sci-fi series called Sanshlian Series. She has also started up an indie publishing company called FoxTales Press. She also works with Anthill Studios in creating comics through Antik Comics.

Her hobbies include reading, watching anime, cooking, studying different languages, wire walking, hula hoop, and working with plants. She is also an herbalist and sells her concoctions on FoxCraft Apothecary. She lives in Phoenix with her husband and visits Seattle often.

Feel free to email her with any questions you might
have!
danihootsauthor@gmail.com